OCT   2001

Coyote
Autumn

Coyote
Autumn

BILL WALLACE

Holiday House/New York

www.holidayhouse.com

First Edition

Library of Congress Cataloging-in-Publication Data

Wallace, Bill, 1947–
Coyote autumn / Bill Wallace. — 1st ed.
p.   cm.
Summary: After moving to the country, thirteen-year-old Brad,
who has always wanted a dog, adopts a motherless coyote.
ISBN 0-8234-1628-3 (hardcover)
[1. Coyotes—Fiction. 2. Dogs—Fiction. 3. Country life—Oklahoma—Fiction.
4. Family life—Oklahoma—Fiction. 5. Oklahoma—Fiction.] I. Title.

PZ7.W15473 Co 2000
[Fic]—dc21   00-022819

To Donna Bigbee and Gerry Willingham
B. W.

Chapter 1

I love days off from school.

Seems like I spent the first half of the school year waiting for Christmas. The second half waiting for spring break.

During the fall, a state teachers' meeting and Thanksgiving broke things up. From New Year's until spring break—there was NOTHING.

Except for today.

Back in Chicago Daddy and I might go ice fishing. But this wasn't one of those times that we could do things together.

The first Friday in February was the only day off between Christmas and spring break. It was free time for us kids, but since Daddy and Mama were both teachers, they were stuck at a conference. Still . . . I had three whole days just to watch TV. I could stay home. I could sleep late.

I love time off from school.

I hate getting up early.

The sheet tangled around my feet. I kicked and flopped over on my stomach. Now I was too cold. I reached down and pulled the covers up. Too hot. So, I flipped the pillow. Cooler.

Just close your eyes and be real still, I thought. Stay quiet for a while. You'll go back to sleep.

Talking to myself didn't work.

I flipped and flopped and twisted and turned. Finally I sat up. It was no use.

My bedroom door squeaked when I opened it. I staggered down the dark hall, through the living room, and into the kitchen.

The refrigerator door *didn't* squeak when I opened it. I took a carton of orange juice to the playroom. There was nothing on the TV but news and a farm report, so I headed to the front porch.

That's the problem with getting up early. Nothing on TV. Nothing to do. Getting up early on a day off from school is about the most boring thing in the world.

At the door, I slipped my moccasins on. Like all doors in our house, this one squeaked when I opened it to get outside. My eyes adjusted to the dim morning light. I plopped down in Mama's lawn chair and took a swig of orange juice.

The February morning was chilly, but not cold. Weird! It was never warm this time of year in Chicago.

Our home was about three hundred yards from the gravel section line road. The front yard was mowed, but beyond the fence there was nothing but weeds and tall grass. Across the road lay a wheat field, and beyond it Tony Hollow Creek. Nolan's dad's alfalfa field bordered the stream. Nolan would have to help his dad with the wheat harvest and the alfalfa, but in between, he said there would be time for fishing and stuff. It sounded like fun.

Another stream was on the far side of the alfalfa field. It was called Tony Hollow Creek, too. That was because they both came together at the pond and made one creek on the far side of the dam.

A movement between the two creeks caught my eye. I squinted. The field was a long ways off. From here I couldn't tell whether something really moved or if I'd just thought it did.

I set down the orange juice and slipped inside. In the dark I felt around on the shelf next to the door for Daddy's binoculars.

I flinched when the door let out its shrill squeak. For a second or two, I listened. Everything was quiet. Once back in the chair, I scanned the area where I'd seen the movement.

My breath caught.

A coyote!

I twisted the wheel on top of the binoculars, trying to bring him into focus. He had brown hair tipped with black, a pointed nose, and sharp ears. His tail was long and bushy.

We'd moved from Chicago to Oklahoma back in August. In the short time we had lived in the country, I'd heard coyotes. They yapped and howled, mostly at sundown. Sometimes, when the trains whistled at the highway crossing, the coyotes howled back. But this was the very first time I ever saw one. He looked a lot like a dog. He walked around, sniffed the ground, trotted a ways, stopped, and sniffed again.

Suddenly another one came into view. This coyote was smaller and not as dark at the tips of its fur. Shorter than the other coyote, it was sort of chubby.

I'd always thought coyotes were scrawny and scraggly looking, but these were sleek. One was even as plump as a little butterball.

When the smaller coyote got to the first one, it cowered, reminding me of Bowzer when Nolan's daddy swatted him for wetting the floor.

The shorter coyote circled the big one a couple of times, then nudged him with its nose. All of a sudden, they ran and played and scampered around the alfalfa field. I was amazed at how fast they moved and how quickly they dodged and changed directions. Then, as suddenly as the game started, it was over. They lay down. The smaller one snuggled up against the big one, without a care in the world, nestling its head on its paw.

Maybe living in the country wasn't so bad

after all. There were things to do and see. No neighbors so close you couldn't even burp without the guy next door calling out, "Excuse you!" It was quiet and peaceful and—

Suddenly, the roar of a motor yanked the quiet and peace right out of my beautiful morning.

Chapter 2

I jerked the binoculars to my eyes so hard it snapped back my head. The only thing I could see on the road was a cloud of dust. But whatever was roaring up the section line was coming fast, really fast.

The two coyotes I had been watching were still in the alfalfa field. Both of them were on their feet now. They seemed nervous. In the blink of an eye, the smaller one took off for the rock hill to the left of the pond like a streak of lightning. The bigger coyote stood alone, eyeing the cloud of dust that swept up the road.

It had been fun watching the coyotes play and romp in the field. Now the fun was over. Some idiot spoiled it by racing on our road.

For half a second, I glimpsed a blue pickup truck. Just as I saw it, it disappeared behind a clump of weeds. A second pickup tore down the road. Then a third. I saw enough of that one to see a metal box on its back. I didn't get a very good look at it—they must have been going sixty miles an hour.

No one ever drove that fast down these gravel roads. Fact was, hardly anybody drove down the road at all. In October I stayed home sick. For three days I only saw five cars.

A fourth pickup came up. This one moved slower than the others and slid to a stop just beyond our mailbox. A man jumped out. He walked quickly around the truck and stopped, facing Nolan's wheat field.

The box on the back was made of metal with slits near the top. I watched the man.

Like me, he had binoculars. He looked out across the field, then suddenly spun back toward his truck. He yanked something on the metal box.

There was a sudden flurry of movement, but from this side of the pickup I couldn't tell what it was. The man raced to my side of the truck and yanked again.

The metal box exploded.

Not really. The doors sprang open and three animals burst out. Tumbling and leaping over one another, they disappeared on the far side of the pickup.

All I could see was a blur of animals racing through the green. The animal in front was a dog, but I'd never seen a dog that skinny and with legs that long.

Eyes tight, I wheeled to the side and tried to see if the lone coyote was still there. He wasn't. He was loping toward the pond—the opposite direction from where the other coyote had gone. It was almost like he *wanted* the dogs to see him. He stopped on the pond dam, long enough to make sure they were still coming. Then he raced down the back side and disappeared.

The six dogs charged across the wheat, bounded over the top of the dam, and vanished. In a second or two, they reappeared in the alfalfa field.

From the corner of my eye, another movement

caught my attention. A pickup bounced across the top of the rock hill to the left of the pond. A man jumped out and six more dogs burst from his truck and into the field.

The first dogs kept running as hard as they could. The pack from the other pickup appeared at the edge of the alfalfa, across from them. Right before the two packs crashed into each other, the lead dogs stopped. A couple of the hounds stumbled over each other and one even slammed into another's rump. Then they sniffed the ground. They sniffed each other. They looked around and started milling about.

Weird.

Nolan would know what all the excitement was. I could hardly wait for him to get here.

Chapter 3

"Wolf hunters."

"Wolf hunters?"

Nolan nodded, looking me square in the eye. Then he blinked.

"Okay, that's what my great-grampa and grampa call 'em." He shrugged. "They're really coyote hunters. Back in the olden days, they really hunted wolves. They went out on a mule or horseback with a pack of greyhounds. When they spotted a wolf, they'd let the dogs loose on 'em.

"Now—there aren't any wolves, just coyotes. They use pickups and two-way radios instead of mules. And the greyhounds ride around in dog boxes."

"Greyhounds?" I asked. "Is that what they were?"

Nolan nodded. "Yeah. They're not good for nothing much except running. But, man, can they run! Anyhow, those guys drive around until they spot some coyotes, then they surround the section. Whoever is closest . . . well, he lets his dogs go, and the chase is on."

I nodded. "I thought they were chasing the coyote, only they weren't. The dogs just met way out there, in the middle of the field, and sniffed one another."

Nolan gave a little chuckle. "They were chasing the coyote, all right. Only coyotes are real crafty. He gave 'em the slip when he went over the pond dam. Greyhounds only hunt by sight."

"Huh?" I frowned.

"Well, their noses don't work too well. They can't follow something by smelling where it went, they can only chase it if they can see it. That old coyote went over the pond dam and hid from 'em. But they just kept running to where they thought he was going. Except when they got there, the coyote was someplace else."

I pointed to the rock hill. "There was another

pickup, there. He let his dogs go, too. At first I thought they might be chasing the fat coyote. Only . . . like . . . is there a whole bunch of coyotes in a pack and they need to have enough dogs to chase all of them?"

Nolan shook his head.

"No. Usually just *one* coyote, but—"

"One?" I yelped. "That's not fair! Twelve dogs against one coyote—"

"But," Nolan held up a finger stopping me. "Those coyotes are quick and sneaky. They're tougher than a greyhound, too. A coyote could whip four of those dogs."

"You ever see it?"

He shook his head.

"Nope. This fella came by one time to ask Daddy if they could hunt on the home place." Nolan glanced around as if someone might be listening. "After the guy left, Daddy told me that those coyote hunters drive like a bunch of idiots."

I nodded.

"Three of them came racing down the road there." I pointed toward the gravel section line. "They were going eighty miles an hour!"

Nolan cocked an eyebrow.

"Okay, not eighty. But sixty."

He motioned toward the front door. "Let's go in and see what's on TV. If it's just junk, we can get your fishing stuff and go to the pond."

"But it's February," I complained.

Nolan frowned at me. "So? This isn't Illinois, Brad. This is Oklahoma. We get warm snaps, even in winter. Might be able to catch some perch or something."

When we walked in, Casey was sitting in his high chair and Mama was doing the dishes. Casey was a total mess. How he could eat cereal and get it and milk in his hair and all over his face—well, it was unbelievable. He held out his arms and grunted. No way was I picking up that kid. I didn't even want to look at him until Mama cleaned off the mess. I brushed past, found the remote, and plopped down on the couch. Even at ten thirty, there was nothing on TV. We headed outside.

The storage barn stood about twenty yards northeast of the house. Its west side was closed in, with shelves and Peg-Boards on the wall. Its east side was open. Mr. Holdbrook, the man we bought the house from, used to keep a horse there.

I wish I had a horse.

Behind the storage barn was a pen built of wire. Mr. Holdbrook had kept his dog there.

I wish I had a dog.

Nolan went inside. I stared at the open part of the barn.

As long as I could remember, we'd lived in apartments. We had one in Chicago, and a larger apartment in Schaumburg. Then we got an even bigger one in Aurora. But none of them had a yard. If I had had a yard, maybe I could have had a horse or a dog.

I would have given anything for a horse. I could see myself, riding across the fields, or exploring the canyons on a beautiful white stallion. But when I'd asked, Mama and Dad had said we couldn't afford a horse.

I would have loved to have a dog.

Dad said that when we got a house, I could have a dog. Only I thought we would always live in an apartment. Then a guy Daddy used to teach with became the superintendent of schools in a little Oklahoma town. He called and asked Daddy to take a job as principal, so we moved to Oklahoma.

Now we had a house. Not only a house, but a house in the country. And, instead of a yard, we had a farm. There was plenty of room for a dog.

But every time I asked, all Mama and Dad said was "We'll see."

I'd love to have a horse or a dog. Shoot—I'd settle for a hamster or a goldfish or . . .

"You okay?"

Nolan's voice snapped me out of my day-dream. He stood smack in front of me holding both fishing rods and my tackle box.

"You okay?" he repeated.

"Sure. Why?"

Nolan shrugged. "Looked like you were off in La La Land or someplace." He shoved the tackle box toward me. "Here. Let's go."

"Brat," Adelee yelled. She, Mama, Daddy, and Casey were beside the car. "Mama wants you."

I hated it when she called me "Brat."

"Brad, the teachers' conference is at the high school," Mama said. "If there's any kind of emergency, Mrs. Bigbee knows the number. Adelee will be at the Morrisons' with Julie, if you can't reach us."

I nodded.

"You and Nolan are going fishing, then over to his house. Is that right?"

"Yes, ma'am."

"You're not going to be playing here, alone, right?"

"Right."

She smiled. "Be careful around that pond."

"We will," I promised.

Chapter 4

Nolan and I threw everything we had at those stupid fish. Nothing so much as wiggled.

After an hour or so, the two of us had worked our way around opposite sides of the pond. That was okay with me. I liked Nolan, but lately he'd been working on his "farmer's blow." Nolan had sinus problems. He was always blowing his nose—only with this "new" technique, he didn't use a Kleenex. He just took a deep breath, leaned over with a finger against one side of his nose, and blew. He was careful not to practice around the house or when grown-ups were near, but once we were alone . . . I mean, it was TOTALLY GROSS!

Even from clear across the pond, I could hear

him blow and snort every now and then. Finally he whistled and motioned toward the dam. We'd left the tackle box on the pipe that stuck out of the ground just above the water. Nolan called it a "tinhorn" and said it was to let the water drain through, so it wouldn't get clear to the top and wash out the dam after heavy rains.

When we sat down, I heard a strange scratching sound. I didn't think about it too long because Nolan handed me two pieces of bubblegum.

"Thanks," I said, popping them in my mouth.

"They're not hitting on artificial lures." He sighed. "We'll have to use bait."

I frowned. "Where do we find bait?"

"It's in your mouth. Stop talking and get busy chewing."

"Bubble gum?"

He nodded. "Just watch." He unwrapped his gum and stuck it in his mouth. Nolan put his Hula Popper back in my tackle box and got out a small hook.

I shoved my wad of gum over in the corner of my jaw and used my front teeth to break the fishing line. Then I dropped the Lucky 13 I'd been using into the tackle box, next to Nolan's plug.

The gum smacked and sloshed as Nolan chased it around his mouth. He kept chomping on it while he tied a hook on his line and one on mine.

Over his smacking sounds, I could hear another noise. It was kind of a scraping or scratching, only I couldn't tell where it was coming from.

With the tip of his tongue, Nolan pushed some bubble gum between his teeth. He pinched it off with his fingers and laid the little wad in the palm of his hand. Then he rubbed his palms together, rolling out the gum like it was Play-Doh or clay. Finally, he had a long, slender string of pink bubble gum.

He held it up by one end and smiled.

"Looks kind of like a worm, don't it?"

I shrugged.

He frowned. "Okay. Well, maybe I got it too skinny." With that, he dropped it back in his hand, took some more gum from his mouth to put with it, and rolled it again.

This time, the stuff *did* look like a worm. Well, sort of. It was pink and it was gum, but if I used a lot of imagination . . . well . . . I guess it had the general shape of a worm.

I did the same with my gum. "This isn't going to work," I mumbled.

"Sure it will." He grinned. "I've caught tons of perch with gum. Bread balls work, too, but we don't have any."

Just as I started rolling the bubble gum in my hand, I heard the scratching sound again. I stopped what I was doing, held my breath, and looked around. I still couldn't tell where it was coming from. With a shrug I added more gum to my "fishing worm."

When the scratching sound came a third time, I snapped my head around—real quick—and glared at Nolan. It had to be him. Sooner or later, I would catch him.

When Nolan saw me staring, he glared back at me.

"What?"

"Did you do that?"

"Do what?"

"That scratching sound. You're doing it, aren't you?" I nodded. "You're doing it all right. Sooner or later I'll catch you."

Nolan's lip curled up on one side. "You're nuts! All I'm doin' is tryin' to get some bait on this hook so I can catch a fish. Why don't you—"

The faint scratching sound made him stop, right in the middle of what he was saying. When we heard it, we both held our breaths, listening. I looked at Nolan. Nolan looked at me. Then, at the exact same instant, we stared at the tinhorn.

"Something's in there," he whispered.

I nodded. Quietly, I lifted my bottom off the dirt and scooted down the hill until I was right beside the opening. Cautiously, I peered in.

There was nothing there. Just dark.

From the corner of my eye, I spotted Nolan scooting himself down the dam toward me.

For some strange reason, I was determined to see what was in there before Nolan did. Holding on for balance, I leaned down so I could look straight into the pipe. Something fuzzy was blocking the hole.

Suddenly, an eye blinked. Not more than two or three feet inside the long pipe, there was a fuzzy, sharp, pointed ear and a long nose and . . . when the eye blinked again, I jumped back.

Nolan was standing over the tinhorn on the other side. The instant I leaped out of the way, he bent over to see what was there.

Only, he never got to look inside.

Just as he stuck his head down, something flew out like a human cannonball, sailed through the air, and landed with a splash at the pond's edge.

Nolan yelled and jumped back. There was a loud clunk when he lit, square on his bottom.

"Coyote!" I yelped. "Did you see him, Nolan? It was the coyote."

Nolan didn't say anything.

He was sitting beside the tinhorn. Well . . . he wasn't exactly sitting. He was kind of like sitting, only he was holding himself up off the ground with his hands and feet. There was a weird look on his face.

"Did you see the coyote?" I asked again.

All Nolan did was bite down on his bottom lip and shake his head.

"What are you doing?"

"Hurting."

"Why?"

"I landed in the tackle box."

"Well, get up and shake it off."

"Can't."

"Why not?"

"Hooks."

Frowning, I walked down the dam toward him. "What do you mean, hooks?"

Still holding himself off the ground with his hands and feet, Nolan winced. "There were hooks in the tackle box. Now they're in my butt."

Chapter 5

The walk to Nolan's house wasn't far. But he flinched and squirmed and moaned with each step.

Getting the fishing hooks out of his bottom was kind of like a major surgery.

First off, Mrs. Bigbee had to get a sharp knife and make tiny incisions in his jeans and Jockey shorts so they could see where the hooks went. Then his dad got a pair of pliers. Every time his mother or his dad touched him, Nolan jumped and yelled. It made me hurt, just thinking about it.

"Barb on this one is into the skin." Mr. Bigbee frowned. "If we try and pull it out, all it's gonna do is tear your hide. We're gonna have to cut the hook and then thread the smooth end through. Grit your teeth, Nolan. This is gonna hurt a little."

Nolan really jumped when his dad used the cutting part of the pliers to snap the hook loose from the plug. The look on his face made me jump, too. If I hadn't been there, I bet Nolan would have cried. I know I would.

"Nolan, you sure it was a coyote?"

Nolan made a gulping sound when he swallowed. "I'm sure. The thing almost ran over me when it jumped out of the—"

While Nolan was talking, Mr. Bigbee sneaked the pliers down and got hold of the very tip of the hook. Quick as snapping your fingers, he looped it through the white skin on Nolan's bottom.

"*YOWIEEeeeee!*"

His dad patted him on the back. "Sorry."

The second hook was about two inches from that one. He warned Nolan when he cut it with the pliers, and before he reached for the end of the hook, he kind of leaned so Nolan could see him.

"Never heard of a coyote hiding inside a pipe. I think maybe you and Brad let your imaginations get away from you."

"I bet it was a dog or a stray cat," Mrs. Bigbee added. "Even a fox, but not a coyote."

"It was a coyote, all right. I'm sure of it. I think he must have hid in there when those dogs were after him. That's how they lost him and— *YOWIEEeeee!*"

Nolan's dad was pretty smart. Every time he was getting ready to pull one of the hooks out, he started an argument about the coyote. Nolan was so busy fussing that he didn't notice his dad sneaking up on the hook. Leastwise, not until it was out.

In fact, once the surgery was over, Mr. Bigbee confessed that he was trying to distract Nolan so it wouldn't hurt so much.

"It was a coyote," he admitted. "I had one of those things climb up and hide in a hay wagon one time. He just jumped on the bed and hid down in the hay bales. 'Bout a minute or two later, here comes this pack of hounds. They raced past the tractor, without even blinking, and went flying over the hill. Once they were gone . . ." Mr. Bigbee let out a little chuckle. "Once they were gone," he repeated, "that old coyote raised up and looked around. I could swear he smiled at me. Then he hopped down and took off in the opposite direction from where the dogs went. Darndest thing I ever saw."

He turned to me. "Brad, you said there were two coyotes when you first spotted them."

"Yes, sir." I nodded. "The other one was kind of short. He was a lot fatter than the one we found in the tinhorn, too."

Mrs. Bigbee nodded. "Probably a female. This is a bit early, but she could be getting ready to have her pups. Those animals never cease to amaze me. For years coyotes have been hunted and trapped and poisoned and chased by hounds—still they're sharp enough to survive. That's what the male was doing. He made sure the dogs came after him instead of the female, then he gave 'em the slip by crawling up inside that pipe. Them coyotes are slick as a whistle." She patted Nolan on the shoulder. I couldn't help but notice the mischievous little twinkle in her eye.

"Next time, close the tackle box before you sit down on it. Okay?"

Nolan's mouth flew open when he looked up at her.

We walked to the living room to watch TV for a while. (Well, I walked. Nolan sort of waddled, real slow and easy.) He lay on his stomach on the couch and I sat on the floor. I'd just got settled when Bowzer came trotting up with his tennis ball. He shoved my hand with his nose, wagged his tail, and raised his head so I could see the ball in his mouth. I took it—slobbers and all—and threw it for him. He raced after it and brought it back. I bounced it off the TV cabinet. He almost turned a somersault when it ricocheted between his front paws. The next time I threw it for him, I managed to angle it off the playroom door. He chased it into the living room.

I couldn't tell which of us was having more fun.

A little after three, Mama called to say they were home from the meeting. She said supper would be ready about five and wanted to know if Daddy should drive over to pick me up.

I told her I'd start about four thirty and walk.

The Bigbees' house was on top of a tall hill about two miles west of our house. We were on top of a big hill, too. The land between belonged to Nolan and his folks. It was a double section— in other words, two sections of land without a road cutting it in half. It was a pretty day and I loved being outside for a change. There were a couple of hills and some pasture, but during the whole walk home, I was never out of sight from either house.

At the pond I stopped and sneaked up on the tinhorn. I peeked in, really quick, and yanked my head back. When nothing moved, I took a closer look. Except for some small branches and a couple of clumps of wet grass and leaves, the big pipe was empty. I looked all around, but there was no sign of the coyotes.

Chapter 6

After dinner, Daddy and I helped Mama clear the table.

"Nathan Holdbrook called, right after we got home from the meeting," Daddy said. "You remember Mr. Holdbrook, the man we bought the house from? Nathan's his son."

I didn't remember him. But before I had a chance to answer, he went on.

"Mr. Holdbrook is living in a retirement home now, up in Kansas. He's having some health problems. Nathan said he wanted to come and visit—see the place one more time before . . . ah . . . well . . . They aren't sure when he'll be feeling well enough to travel, but I really want it to look nice for the old man. So tomorrow and the next few weekends you will have to help me do some cleaning and straightening up outside."

"But Nolan and I had talked about going fishing tomorrow and—"

"After." Daddy smiled. His voice was firm when he cut me off. "After we're done around the house."

Sunday, after church, Daddy and I chopped weeds and cleaned out the dog pen behind the shed.

Cleaning out a dog pen seemed like a good time to ask again.

"My birthday isn't long after spring break," I said. "I'm going to be thirteen."

Daddy didn't say anything.

"Remember . . . last year? Remember me asking for a dog? The apartment didn't have a yard. But now . . . we've got a big yard. We even have a dog pen."

Daddy still didn't say anything.

I raked awhile longer, then stopped and leaned on my rake handle. "What do you think, Daddy? Wouldn't a dog be fun?"

"We'll see." Then he gave his long talk about how much responsibility a dog was and all that stuff. I promised him that I was old enough to take care of a dog, so he changed the subject and started talking about something else.

The following two Saturdays, I slept late. Daddy and I restacked the woodpile so it looked neat and chopped weeds out in what used to be the horse lot. The next weekend we hauled off a bunch of junk and trash that was piled up behind the shed. The Saturday after that, we pruned the trees in the front yard and cut back the lilac hedge beside the driveway. It was hard work, and not nearly as much fun as fishing.

Well, so much for Saturdays.

I guess there was always school.

Having parents who were both teachers wasn't easy. It did have its good points, though. Best of all was we didn't have to ride the school bus. Mama taught fifth-grade math at the Intermediate School. That's where Nolan and I went. We were in sixth grade, though. Each morning we picked up Nolan and drove four miles into Chickasha. Mama went inside to visit with the other teachers and drink her coffee. Nolan and I had time to visit and play with our friends before the bell rang.

I have to admit, at first I was a little scared about moving to Oklahoma. I mean, I had been in new schools before and knew that it took two to three weeks to make friends. It wasn't easy, but I knew I could handle it. Oklahoma—that was a whole different world from Chicago. Nolan found me the first day, and when he discovered that we were the ones who moved into the old Holdbrook place, he became my best friend, right off. Other than my accent, I felt like I fit in here quicker and easier than anyplace I had ever been. I couldn't figure why they thought my accent was funny, though. I mean *they* were the ones who talked different.

I liked school, but I was *sure ready* for spring break.

Saturday morning—the first day of spring break, I couldn't sleep. I went out on the front porch. Some of the coyote hunters went tearing up the road in their trucks, but I never saw any coyotes. Not long after I went back inside, Mama got up and started fixing breakfast. Daddy's bare feet plopped across the tile floor when he staggered in and went to the coffeepot. Just about the time he had his coffee fixed, the phone rang. When he hung up, he told us that Nathan Holdbrook called and his dad was feeling well enough to travel. They would be here next weekend.

Well . . . there went spring break.

Daddy and I painted the trim around the house, edged the sidewalk out front, spread gravel in our driveway, and dug the grass out of the flower beds. Friday—my last day of *real* spring break— we raked leaves in the front yard.

Back in November, we cleaned out the rain gutters and raked leaves, but more fell from the trees or blew in. Something was always blowing into our yard—from someplace.

When we had an enormous pile in the front yard, Daddy let Casey come out and romp in it.

It irritated me a little, at first. I mean, it took a bunch of work to get all those leaves piled up. But Casey squealed and giggled and had such a time, I couldn't help but dive in and join him after a while. We leaped and tumbled.

Nolan showed up about the time we were done. He said we might as well go fishing. We headed for the shed to get our stuff, but hadn't gotten our things together when the clap of thunder cracked. Huge blue-green clouds raced toward us from the west.

We heard a car. Nolan's mom slid her Oldsmobile to a stop in our gravel driveway.

"Nolan," she called. "Get in the car. Quick! There are tornado warnings. We've got to get home."

Nolan noticed the look on my face. "Don't get all in a sweat," he whispered. "It's probably nothing. It's too cool for tornados. We don't get them in March, usually." I didn't like the way he added *usually*. "Mama's just like this."

"Nolan! *Now!*"

"Yes, ma'am." He winked at me. "Tomorrow morning, I'll meet you at the pond."

"Nolan! Right this instant. I mean it!"

They drove away. I stood there, staring wide-eyed at the clouds that rolled toward our home.

Twister. The thought spun round and round in my head like a funnel cloud.

Chapter 7

Twister!

No matter how hard I tried to make myself think about other things—it was the only vision that kept popping into my head. I wished Daddy had never bought that stupid movie, and I wished I'd never watched it on our VCR.

Each time the wind shook the shutters, I jumped up and looked. Mama and Daddy made me get away from the windows. When the limbs on the trees rattled and hissed, I could almost hear the roar of a tornado. I had to go look again. I got yelled at again, too.

There was a bunch of lightning and a lot of wind when the storm first started. Now, there was only rain. But this rain wasn't like Chicago rain. This rain was *rain!* Rain that rumbled.

Rain so thick, I couldn't see Tony Hollow. It came at us like a wall.

The rain kept going and going. It was dark when we sat down for supper. Adelee was all excited about a phone call she got. One of her friends, who was also on her soccer team, called to say the game on Saturday was canceled. They were going to make it up next week, by playing two games. That meant that some of the younger girls, like Adelee, would get to play. Adelee was so hyper, she kept bouncing and wiggling in her chair until I thought it was going to break.

I kind of ignored her and kept thinking about the two coyotes. It had been six weeks—six *long* weeks—since I had last seen them. Even so, the vision of them romping and playing was still fresh in my mind. If coyotes could be that fun and sweet, just imagine . . .

"Can I have a dog?"

The words sort of tumbled out of my mouth. Everybody stopped eating and just stared at me. With a sheepish smile, I kind of shrugged and asked again. (This time a lot softer than before.)

"Can I have a dog, Daddy?"

"What are you going to do with a dog?" Adelee asked before Daddy could say anything. She crinkled her nose. "You can't even clean your room. You don't ever do anything. You wouldn't take care of a dog if you had one. The thing would end up starving to death or smelling as bad as your room does. Maybe worse."

I glared at her. She glared back. Adelee had practiced her glare more than I had. She had a nastier, meaner look.

"Why don't you go out for sports or something, Brat?" I hated that, and she knew it. "All you ever do is sit around and play with that stupid PlayStation or watch TV or—"

"That's enough, Adelee," Mama said. "There's no need for you to be mean to your little brother all the time."

"But Brat never does anything," Adelee argued. "Brat just sits around and—"

"Brad helped me with the yard and the woodpile," Daddy said. "I don't remember seeing you anyplace around when it came time for yard work."

"I had soccer practice."

"Every day?" I tried to ask with the same snotty voice she used on me.

Daddy plopped his fork on the table so hard, our glasses rattled. "That's enough! Both of you!"

Adelee and I ducked our heads and stared at our plates. Daddy sat quiet for a while, then cleared his throat.

"About the dog." His voice was a lot softer now. "We'll see." That was all he said.

After supper I went to my room and put a CD in my PlayStation. By nine thirty I still wasn't sleepy. I hadn't done anything all day but stay away from Adelee. Thinking about the coyotes cheered me up some. I went to bed. The way I felt, right now, watching coyotes with Daddy's binoculars was probably as close as I would ever get to having a pet of my own.

The loud, sudden screech startled me. I sat straight up in bed and whacked the button on top of the alarm. The screeching stopped.

When the early morning haze cleared from my head, I kicked my way out of bed and staggered over to the dresser. I pulled on my sweatpants, a pair of socks, and tucked in my pajama tops. I gritted my teeth when the door squeaked. Then I got orange juice, found Daddy's binoculars, and plopped in the chair on the front porch.

When I saw the coyotes standing at the edge of the alfalfa field, my smile crinkled up my face so much that I couldn't even use the binoculars. I pulled them away and wriggled my face back to normal. The coyotes romped and played—just like the last time I watched them. The little one chased the big one, then he chased her. Puddles of water stood in Nolan's alfalfa field. The spray shot high in the air when they raced through them. Sometimes, they even bit at the water droplets as they ran. It was so much fun to watch them. It made me feel good inside, only I don't know why. Maybe it was normal or natural or something like that. Maybe it was the way things were supposed to be—animals frolicking free and wild and . . .

Suddenly, both of them stopped.

I held my breath, listening. There was nothing.

But in a second or two, I heard the roar of a motor. This time, only one truck raced up our road. It slid to a stop, just across from our mail-box. Before it was even through sliding on the muddy road, a man leaped out and opened both sides of the dog box.

When I turned back to look at the coyotes, the little one slipped under the fence and headed toward the trees on the rock hill. The big one strolled, without a care in the world, toward the pond. He stopped, just like last time. Once he was sure the greyhounds were watching him, he disappeared over the dam.

That was one smart coyote. He had them again. They'd never look for him in that drain-pipe. I couldn't believe my eyes when he sud-denly appeared on the far side of the pond dam.

"What are you doing?" I yelped. "Hide in the tinhorn—the drainpipe. They'll see you!"

He ran for the open field. The greyhounds were almost to the dam.

Chapter 8

I don't remember leaping from the chair. I don't remember running out into the middle of the yard. Only when I hit one of the barbs on the pasture fence, did I realize where I was.

"Run!" I urged. "That's it. Run!"

I couldn't believe how fast he was. But the dogs were faster. It was like watching arrows fly at a target.

A knot tightened in my throat.

The lead dog caught up with the coyote just before he got to the fence at the far side of the field. He slammed into him. Both went tumbling. Before either could get up, the second greyhound smashed into the coyote, too. His open mouth reached for the coyote's neck.

The coyote snarled and snapped. White fangs

44

slashed the air like swords. Somehow, he managed to get to his feet. The second dog jumped back. But before the coyote could run, the lead dog grabbed his hind leg. The coyote turned on him. As soon as he did, the other dog leaped in again.

Strong jaws closed on the dog's neck. The coyote yanked him and threw him to the ground. Then he turned to the other one and lashed out. In the blink of an eye, the coyote turned for the fence one last time to make his escape.

But the other four dogs were there now. Snarling, biting, slashing, tearing . . .

I couldn't watch.

When Nolan had told me the greyhounds chased the coyotes . . . well . . . I thought that was what they did—*chased* coyotes. It never dawned on me that they might catch them. And if they caught them . . . even in my worst nightmares, I never dreamed of a sight as horrible as the one before me.

My insides were tied in knots.

The man started out running, then jogged. Now, he walked across the dam. The six dogs stood in a circle, but the snarling and biting were over. A limp, still, brown heap lay in the center of their circle. I didn't want to see it closer.

My heart felt like a heavy rock inside my chest. I started to turn for the house. Suddenly, four of the dogs burst from the circle and tore across the field to the left.

I swung the binoculars, trying to find them. Once I could tell where their noses were aimed, I scanned ahead. For the second time, that hard, heavy feeling came inside the middle of my chest.

It was the other coyote.

Two more dogs were hot on her heels. From the corner of my eye, I saw a second pickup parked on top of the rock hill. The doors to the dog box were open. I held my breath. Watched—hoping and praying—until the first dog hit her.

I ran to the house, closed the squeaky door behind me, and locked it.

Nobody seemed to care.

When I tried to tell Mama, all she said was: "That's terrible. Put Casey in his high chair for me, will you?"

Daddy shook his head and said: "I'm sorry you had to see it. It sounds horrible. By the way, Mr. Holdbrook is coming tomorrow morning. I need you to help me clean off the front porch, sometime today."

I didn't even get to tell Adelee. Not that she would have cared, either. I'd just started when the phone rang. She raced to it. Her face kind of lit up and she began jabbering and wrapping herself in the cord.

Nobody seemed to care.

"They're just coyotes." That's all Nolan had to say when we finally met at the pond around ten.

I glared at him.

"But . . . it's . . . it's not right," I stammered. "I mean, one minute, all they were doing was playing in the field and minding their own business. Then, all of a sudden—for no reason— these guys and their dogs come tearing up and . . . well . . . they . . . they . . . I mean, the poor coyotes weren't doing anything!"

Nolan flipped his plug into the water.

"Coyotes are always doin' something. They

get people's chickens. Coyotes will even pull down and eat baby calves. They're just vermin."

With that, he strolled away toward the far corner of the dam to cast his plug at another spot. I looked down at the tinhorn below me. Today, water was clear up over the top of it, swirling and gurgling as it rushed through the pipe and into the creek on the other side.

"No wonder." I sighed. "That's why he couldn't hide there. The water from yesterday's rain was pouring through the pipe and . . . and . . ."

Fishing wasn't fun. Usually, fishing got my mind off stuff. When I was fishing, that's all I thought about. All the other things—all the problems or the worries—just went away. Not today.

I walked way up the channel, found a big tree and plopped down under it. I just sat there, staring at the water.

That's when I heard the sound.

Chapter 9

The sound was hard to describe. It was kind of a whining—only it wasn't. More of a high, shrill squeak, it reminded me of the doors in our house. Only this squeaking kept going and going.

The sound led me up the channel. The pond was full, its brown water churning and swirling. The bank was muddy and slippery in spots.

Now the squeaking was coming from above and behind me. It lasted only a moment or two, then quieted. The bank was steep here—almost a straight drop to the water if I slid. I went on a little farther, until I found a more gentle slope that didn't look so treacherous. Using tufts of grass and small trees to help pull me up the muddy slope, I slipped and slid and dragged myself to the edge.

That's when the sound started again. I froze, listening. It came from my left—back toward the dam. It was close—very close.

A few steps brought me to the edge of a little clearing. When a movement caught my eye, I froze. I didn't breathe. I didn't blink. I didn't even move my eyes. Not at first. When the squeaking sound came again, my glance darted straight to a baby coyote.

He sat near the middle of the clearing. He whined and whimpered and made that squeaking noise. There was something in front of him. I had to blink to see what it was.

Then I blinked again and again, trying to fight back the tears.

It was another baby coyote. Only this one lay on the ground. Its fur was wet. Its little body was limp and mangled. It was dead.

Nolan had told me there were usually five or six dogs. But when I'd seen the female coyote at the edge of the alfalfa field, only two dogs were chasing her.

She made a beeline for the den, but she never made it. Two of the hounds went for her. The others must have stumbled on to the pups and . . . and . . .

My lips clamped together as tight as they could. I pulled my eyes away from the pitiful sight. But that only made things worse. When I looked away, there was another little coyote. And another and another. Four all together, scattered near the opening to the den.

A tear leaked out and rolled down my cheek. It was the saddest, most gut-wrenching sight I ever saw in my life, and—

"Brad? Brad, where are you?"

Nolan's voice was far off. The baby coyote heard him, too. He sprang to his feet and took a couple of steps toward the den in the middle of the clearing.

It's amazing how fast a mind works.

He thought his den was safe, a place where nothing could hurt him. But his mama and daddy were dead. His brothers and sisters were dead, too. He was alone. If he made it to that hole, he would die.

All that thinking and figuring what he was thinking and thinking what I had to do . . .

51

well . . . like I said, it's amazing how fast a mind works. It all took about as long as it takes a hummingbird's wings to flap.

I was already at a dead-out sprint toward the hole before the little coyote broke and ran.

It was a good thing. His short little puppy legs were fast. I ran as hard as I could. So did he.

We neared the den at about the same time. How I got my coat in front of me—I don't know. Holding it by the shoulders, I dove. It stretched out like a sail. I landed flat on my stomach.

The impact kind of knocked the air out of me. I didn't know whether I had him or not.

There was a lump under my jacket.

It moved.

Chapter 10

Nolan was standing by the tree where I left my fishing rod, staring down at the murky brown water.

"Whatcha looking at?" I called.

Startled, he jumped and wheeled on me. When he did, his foot slipped in the mud. He plopped down so hard on his bottom that he bounced.

"Where have you been?" he demanded, struggling back to his feet. "Why didn't you answer me? You scared me to death! I found your fishing rod, but you were no place around. Then I thought about how slippery the bank was and how much water's pouring into the pond and . . ." He stopped snarling at me and looked down. "What's in your coat?"

Then his head kind of snapped back. His nose crinkled up until his eyes were nothing but tiny slits.

"What's that smell?!"

Nolan made me lead the way back to the dam. That's because the breeze was coming from behind us and he made me stay upwind.

He threw my rod down beside the tackle box and wheeled to face me. "They're gonna kill you!"

I shrugged.

"Why?"

He sneered at the coat, bundled gently in my arms.

"That's why!"

"Daddy's been saying I could have a dog and—"

"That's not a dog!" He cut me off. "It's a coyote."

"But it's just a puppy."

"It's a coyote!"

"It's a puppy. He'll starve if I don't—"

"It's a coyote puppy, and when your mother gets a look at that coat . . ." He rolled his eyes and shook his head. "They're gonna kill you. No way around it. You're dead!"

I snuggled the coat tighter against my tummy.

"It wasn't his fault. What would you do if some huge monster came flying at you, threw a coat over your head, and wrapped you up? It would have scared the poop out of you, too. Wouldn't it?"

All Nolan did was shake his head.

"Yeah. But when she sees that coat . . ."

"Well, I'll just tell her it's mud."

"Mud?" Nolan yelped. "Hate to tell you this, but mud don't smell like that!"

I shrugged.

"Well, I'll have to think of a way where she won't see it or smell it. She's got this stuff that she soaks Adelee's soccer things in. I could get that and—"

"You don't think they're gonna *smell* it—the second you walk into the house?"

"Okay. I could get that old bucket out in the dog pen, clean it out, and pour in the stuff. Once the poop is out, I could sneak my coat into the washing machine."

Nolan just rolled his eyes. "When they see

you've brought home a coyote, they're gonna flip."

"So, they just won't see it."

"Yeah, right!"

"Really," I insisted. "I can keep him in the dog pen. Nobody ever goes out there. He could stay for months, and they wouldn't even know he was around."

"What are you gonna feed him?"

I smiled.

"That's where *you* come in."

Nolan's eyes flashed. "Count me out. I'm not—"

"He's got to have something to eat," I began. "I know you've got some food for Bowzer. Sneak some of it out of the house and bring it over."

"Sneak dog food?"

"Yeah. We can't let anybody know about it."

"You're crazy!"

"I know."

"No, really. You can't keep a coyote. They're not like a dog. They're wild. Wild animals . . . You're crazy!"

I looked Nolan square in the eye.

"Don't let anybody see you bringing the dog

food. Sneak in around the north side of the shed and put it in the old hay barn before you come to the door, okay?"

I made sure the gate to Mr. Holdbrook's dog pen was latched behind me before I loosened my grip on the coat. If I unwrapped him, it would probably just scare him and he was scared enough as it was. So I just carefully placed the bundle on the ground and stepped away.

For a long time, the coat just lay there. Then there was a little wiggle. Suddenly a brown fuzzball burst from underneath, glanced up at me, and took off in the opposite direction.

Smack-dab into the fence!

There was a thunk. The force threw him backward. He rolled over, scrambled to his feet, and raced off again—smack-dab into the fence at the far side of the pen.

Slowly and carefully, I backed out, closed the gate, and slipped around the edge of the shed. Once out of sight, I stopped and listened.

The thunk sound didn't come again, but I could still hear his little paws racing back and forth. I eased up to the edge of the woodpile and peeked around. The baby coyote had stopped running. He sniffed and shoved with his little nose as he checked out every inch of the fence.

Behind me, I heard the front door slam. I lunged for the gate, grabbed my tackle box and fishing rod, and hopped to the middle of the driveway. Letting my shoulders sag and leaning my head down, I tried my best to look tired.

Daddy peeked out the front door.

"Mom almost has lunch ready. You catch anything?"

My knees locked. How could he know about the coyote?

I looked dumb.

"Huh?"

Daddy frowned at me. "Fish. Did you catch any fish?"

"No, sir. Didn't even get a bite."

He nodded toward the shed. "Put your fishing stuff up and come help me move this lawn furniture. Where's your coat?"

I was good at dumb looks. I gave him the very dumbest one I had and said, "What coat?"

It worked.

Chapter 11

Daddy fussed at me for not taking my coat. I told him it was really warm and I hadn't needed one. (Which was true—only I didn't tell him I *did* take a coat. I didn't really lie, I just didn't tell all the truth . . . sort of.)

After lunch, Adelee called one of her friends on the phone, Mama started cleaning up Casey, and Daddy plopped himself in front of the TV. It was the perfect time.

I sneaked down the hall to the utility closet. The cleaning stuff was in the cabinet above the washing machine. Only problem—instead of one bottle, there were four. They were all about the same size, but different, too. Frowning, I pulled each down and studied it.

Clorox, Biz, Woolite, Wisk . . . I wished I'd paid more attention.

I grabbed the Clorox bottle and headed for the door. Outside, I stooped down and crept under the kitchen window. Not that Adelee would have noticed. The TV room had a big picture window. I got down on my hands and knees to get under that one. Not that Daddy would look up. The Bulls and the Knicks were playing. Still, Mama or Casey might spot me.

Once clear, I scurried to the pen. When I got there, my heart sank clear down into my socks.

The coyote pup was gone!

Frantic, I dropped the bottle and rushed to the pen. There had to be a hole in the wire. Maybe he hadn't gotten too far. I studied every inch of the pen, but couldn't find any gaps or holes in the chain link. There was no fresh dirt from something digging.

An old, plastic doghouse stood on the far side of the pen, nestled near the horse barn. Once it had been white, now it was dingy looking. Quiet as a cat sneaking up on a mouse, I eased toward it and leaned down to peek inside.

He was there, pressed against the back wall, trembling like I did when I had the chills. His little feet scratched the floor as he tried to push himself away from me.

I stooped, shaking my head. *Take care of your coat first,* I told myself. *Keep Mama from killing you. Then you can worry about him.*

The rubber bucket was totally grungy. I turned it upside down to spill out the yucky brown water. Then I took it to the faucet, rinsed it out, and rubbed it as clean as I could.

I hid the bucket behind Daddy's lawn mower in the horse barn. Nobody would look there. I stuffed the smelly red coat in it and poured in some of the Clorox. Then I poured in some more, just in case.

I took a long piece of wood from the woodpile and poked the coat until it was under the Clorox. Satisfied, I headed back to the baby coyote.

A round tin building with a cone-shaped top was about five or ten yards from the dog pen. It reminded me of the Amish silos near Goshen, Indiana. Only this building was metal and shorter. I'd looked in it before, when we first moved here, but couldn't remember what was there.

There were three bales of hay inside. The one to my left was sort of a half bale, with the wire cut and part of it loose on the floor. It looked almost white in the dim light. The other two were darker. The whole floor was covered with loose hay.

I scooped up an armload and headed outside. A gust of wind caught the door. I saw it swinging shut, but before I could do anything . . .

WHAM!

It was suddenly as dark as night. When the door slammed, the tin barn banged and vibrated so loud, I thought I was standing inside a bell. Dropping the hay, I scrambled for the door, flung it open, and leaped outside.

"What are you doing?"

I jumped. Nolan stood just outside the barn, smiling.

"What are you doing?" he repeated.

"Getting hay for the doghouse."

He looked down at my hands. "Hay?"

"Okay . . . I . . . ah . . . I dropped some."

"Oh."

I motioned to the tin barn with my head. "Just hold the door." I scooped up another armload.

Nolan had a feed sack in his right hand. He set it beside the door and shook his head. "What you got in your hand is alfalfa. Not much good for bedding. Any straw or grass hay in there?"

He noticed my blank look. "You hold the door. I'll check."

The white-looking bale was grass hay. He got two big chunks of it and put it on the ground. Then he opened the feed sack.

It was about half full of dry dog food with five cans on top of that. Nolan lined up the cans just inside the door. Then he dug in his pocket and pulled out a can opener. He set the sack next to the cans.

"Little guy's probably hungry," he said. "Why don't we feed him, first. Then we can fix his house."

Neither one of us had ever fed a coyote puppy before. . . .

Chapter 12

Nolan remembered seeing an old pan that Mr. Holdbrook used to feed his bird dog. When he couldn't find it in the pen, he went into the barn to look.

I took the can opener and tried to open one. I was still working on it when Nolan came back with a plastic bowl. He snorted, took the can opener from me, and mumbled something about "dumb city kid."

"Well, we never had one of those," I confessed. "The only thing we use are electric can openers."

He snorted again. Then he showed me how to use it.

Once the can was open, Nolan poured some

of the dry dog food into the bowl. Next, he dumped the canned food on top of it.

"You'll need to sneak a knife from the house. That way you can chop up the canned meat and mix it in with the dry. That's what we do with Bowzer."

He wanted to see the coyote, so we went inside the pen. I set the bowl down a little ways from the opening of the doghouse. Both of us stepped back.

Nothing happened.

Nolan went over and peeked inside.

"Is he still there?"

"Yeah. He ain't doin' nothin', though. Just sittin' and shakin'."

Nolan shoved the bowl a little closer to the opening. Then he came to stand beside me at the fence.

"I was afraid of this," I whispered. "He's too scared to eat."

"Maybe he doesn't know what it is," Nolan said. "I mean, he's probably never seen a dog bowl before. Maybe if he can smell it or see it . . . Maybe if he gets a taste of it . . ."

I walked over to kneel down beside the doghouse. The puppy cowered in the dark shadows. He growled at me.

It wasn't a very convincing growl. It didn't even sound mean—just scared.

"I'm not going to hurt you."

He growled again.

Even growling, he was cute as could be. He had a pointed nose with a little black tip on the end. His ears were sharp and stuck straight up, until he growled. Then they lay down flat against his head. His face was lighter than the rest of him, and his back and sides were dark, with blackish hairs that stuck out above the brown. His fur looked as soft as one of Mama's sweaters. The tips of his paws were white.

"Come on," I coaxed. "Try some of this. You'll like it."

His little brown eyes glared at me—not the food.

I stuck my hand into the yucky stuff and pinched off some.

He growled again. I shoved the meat off my fingertips and yanked my hand back. His little black nose wiggled. He leaned toward the food, still sniffing, but his eyes never left mine. His pointed ears went straight up, and his neck stretched even farther toward the little chunk of meat.

At last, his eyes left me. He glanced down at the meat. I blinked.

The meat was gone!

The puppy wasn't chewing or licking his lips or anything. He just sat there, glaring up at me. But the meat was gone.

I pinched off another chunk. I'd watch better this time.

The second it left my fingertips, he lunged, then gobbled it down in one gulp.

I pinched off some more meat, but before I set it down, I tilted the bowl, thinking that if he could *see* the food inside . . .

The pup leaped. I yanked my hand back so fast I clunked myself square in the chest. Before I had time to make sure my fingers were okay, he leaped again.

He stood with all four feet in the bowl, gobbling and snapping at the food like he was starving to death. He didn't even bother to chew—he just scarfed it down. We watched him, then Nolan suggested that if I moved the dog bowl, we could put the hay in his doghouse so it would be all ready for him.

When the puppy saw me coming, he snarled. I took another step. He gave a little hop, spreading out his front legs like he was trying to surround the food. He let me know—real quick—that it was *his* food and he'd guard it with his life.

I couldn't help but laugh. I glanced over my shoulder at Nolan.

"*You* move the food bowl. I'll get the hay."

He didn't laugh. We ended up leaving the food bowl right where it was. Nolan handed the hay over the fence, and I draped myself over the top of the doghouse and stuffed it in, one handful at a time. We were done before the puppy left the food bowl. He licked the bowl so clean, it looked like it came fresh from the dishwasher.

We made it to my room without anyone seeing us. Mama came in to tell me dinner was ready. She was surprised to see Nolan and asked when he came in. He said he hadn't been here very long.

After we ate, everyone settled down. Daddy fell asleep on the couch with Casey on his chest. Mama started grading papers, but she dozed off, too. Adelee got on the phone.

Nolan and I sneaked out to the barn. Holding my breath, I pulled my coat from the bucket. There was still a little coyote poop on it, so I scrubbed it like Mama did with grass stains. Then I sloshed it in the bucket, squeezed out the liquid, and rinsed it.

There was already a load of clothes in the washing machine. I put the coat in and hid it under all the white stuff. Even then, I was a little worried that Mama might see it when she started the water.

I felt good when I went to bed that night. I had had my new coyote almost a whole day, and no one knew he was around. If I could get him really tame . . . well . . . Mama and Daddy would *have* to let me keep him.

Chapter 13

Sunday after church, we ate dinner at Eduardo's Mexican Restaurant. Adelee met one of her soccer friends and asked if she could go home with her. Mama and Daddy said okay.

When we got back to the house, I played with Casey while Mama went to start the wash. I held my breath the whole time she was in the utility room. When she came back and started grading papers, I was so relieved that the air just whooshed out of me. I was home free!

Once everyone was settled, I sneaked a knife from the kitchen, then slipped outside.

I opened the hay silo. It was still a pain to work the can opener, but I finally managed and mixed the food with the knife.

Latching the gate behind me, I eased up to the doghouse. I paused a moment, then put the food bowl near the doorway and waited.

When nothing happened, I peeked inside. The coyote pup was squished against the wall, shivering and trembling. I scooted the dog food closer to the opening.

"Come on," I coaxed. "I'm not going to hurt you. Come and eat your dinner."

That's all it took.

He landed smack-dab in the middle of the bowl. Feet spread apart, protecting his food, he glared up at me and growled.

He started gobbling it down, not even chewing. He just grabbed and swallowed, keeping a watchful eye on me all the time. I simply stood there—not easing closer or threatening him in any way, but not hiding from him or running off, either.

"You don't need to be scared." I talked to him, real soft and gentle. "I've always wanted a pet, and you're it. But you're supposed to play with a pet. You know, roughhouse and hug and snuggle and all that stuff. You keep growling at me, it's really hard to even think about hugging you."

He looked up and growled again. It was a little growl and not very scary.

I heard another noise—the rumble of a car. I darted to the gate. Slipping through, I latched it behind me, then sprinted to the front porch. Once there, I plopped down in Mama's lawn chair.

My bottom barely hit the wood slats when the door creaked open. Frowning, Mama looked down at me.

I smiled at her. "Hi. What's up?" I tried to sound innocent.

Mama's eyes got tight.

"A blur just went flying past the playroom window. Was that you?"

I nodded, chased the smile from my face and tried to look concerned. "Yeah. There's a car coming up the driveway. I didn't know who it was."

Mama stepped outside and leaned so she could see around the side of the house. From the sound of the motor, the car was getting close. I could hear the tires grinding on the gravel.

"Well, it's not the Grissams' car. Not the Bigbees', either." She went back to the door and pulled it open. "Darrel!" she called to Daddy. "Darrel, get up. Somebody's here."

Daddy came to the door, holding Casey. He handed Casey to Mama and, still half asleep, waddled to the sidewalk.

"Think it's Mr. Holdbrook and his son," he called over his shoulder.

A young man with black hair got out the driver's side of the car. He smiled and shook hands with Daddy. They visited a moment, then Daddy walked around to the passenger side while the young man went to open the trunk.

Daddy reached in and shook hands with someone. I couldn't tell who he was visiting with, because the car windows were so dark. Whoever it was, there was no rush to get out of the car.

The young guy brought a metal walker around to the door where Daddy stood. He set the walker in front of the door. Then, they stood there for a long, long time.

Finally, a cap, with white hair sticking out from under it, appeared. Then a blue work shirt and overalls. The old man took forever to get out. Slowly, he unfolded, stood, and held on to the bars of his walker.

Daddy and the young man walked on either side of Mr. Holdbrook as he toddled up the sidewalk. When they finally got to the porch, Daddy introduced Mama and then Casey and me. The younger man was named Nathan. Only he really wasn't all that young—he was probably as old as Daddy. He just looked young, compared to his father.

Mr. Holdbrook shook hands with us. His hand felt frail when I shook it, but hard and strong, too. When Daddy introduced Casey, the old man smiled and reached out his trembling, withered hand and touched Casey as gently as if he were touching a baby bird. Then, scooting his walker in front of him, he shuffled over to the old rocking chair in the corner.

Daddy asked if they would like something to drink. When he went inside to fix a Coke for Nathan and a glass of milk for Mr. Holdbrook, Mama excused herself and went to put some fresh clothes on Casey. On her way inside, she told them to make themselves at home and asked me to keep them company.

"Good lookin' coyote pup," the old man blurted out.

My mouth fell open.

Chapter 14

I just knew Mama was going to come back through the door. She'd fold her arms, pat her foot, and say: "*What* coyote pup?"

But Mama didn't come back.

Old Mr. Holdbrook must have noticed the look on my face. He frowned at me, then cleared his throat.

"They ain't seen the coyote yet?"

I shook my head.

He shook *his* head.

"You're downright stupid if you don't tell 'em. They're gonna find out sooner or later and—"

"That's not very polite, Dad," Nathan interrupted.

"What ain't?"

"You said he was stupid if—"

"Ain't got time to be polite," Mr. Holdbrook snapped. "Already lived two months longer than them doctors told me I would. Take time to be polite, I'll be dead 'fore I get stuff said what needs said."

He looked back at me.

"Like I was saying, it's stupid not to tell 'em. They're gonna spot him and it's better if they hear it from you instead of just stumbling on to him. Surprised they ain't seen it already."

"I just caught him yesterday."

"Handled him yet?"

"No, sir. Thought I'd give him some time to get used to me, first, then—"

"Don't work that way," he snapped. "Wait for a coyote pup to gentle down, it don't never happen. Got any welding gloves?"

"Huh?"

"Welding gloves. Guess not. Know the Bigbees?"

"Yes, sir. Nolan's my best friend. He was with me when we found the coyote. We were—"

"Paul Bigbee's got welding gloves. Put on a pair of regular leather gloves, then put on the welding gloves over them. They're long enough to cover most of your arm. Then chase down that pup, latch onto him, and start petting him and rufflin' his hair and downright mauling him around.

"He's gonna bite you. You can bet your butt on that. But the gloves ought to keep those sharp, puppy teeth from breaking the skin. Just don't let him get hold of somethin' what ain't covered.

"Ought to take two to three times 'fore he settles down and lets you pick him up and pet him. Soon as you got him calm enough so you can handle him without the gloves, put them back on and have your dad take you to a vet name of Traylor, up in Oklahoma City. Harry's used to workin' with wild critters. Coyote will need puppy shots, a heartworm check, and a rabies vaccination."

"That's a *lot* to remember."

The old man's eyes crinkled up on the sides. I bet there were a hundred lines beside each one. "Ain't that much. Fact is—never mind, except for the handling part. Traylor will know what to do."

"Can I ever make a good pet out of him?"

"You got less than a fifty-fifty chance. Had two. Caught Doofus when I was about fourteen. He was fun when he was little, but when he matured, got surly and mean. Just up and wandered off one day. Never did see him again. Scooter . . . well, shoot . . . reckon I was in my twenties or so when I caught him. He settled down right good. You couldn't tell the difference between him and the dogs. He stayed close to the house. Other coyotes would get to singing of an evening and he'd howl back—but never left the place. Had him about the time I got Slim. Best darned bird dog I ever owned. Thought about making a bird dog out of Scooter, too. But I was so busy farming that I didn't have the time it takes to train him."

He glanced off at the sky for a moment. I couldn't help but notice the faraway look in his eye.

"That coyote pup will be the best pet you ever had *and* the worst."

The best *and* the worst? He must have meant the best *or* the worst. It couldn't be both.

I started to ask him about it, only right then

the front screen opened. Mama had put Casey's yellow jumper on him and washed his face. Daddy handed Nathan a Coke and took a glass of milk to Mr. Holdbrook.

"Sorry it took us so long," Daddy apologized. "You gentlemen find much to visit about while we were gone?"

Mr. Holdbrook shot his son a stern look, as if telling him to shut up. The younger man nodded. Mr. Holdbrook smiled. "Nothing much," he lied. "Just fixing to tell Brad about this old rocking chair and my bird dog, Slim. He was a pointer—mostly white with lemon ears and a spot near his tail. Big ole head and square shoulders. Rascal could smell a bird a half mile away."

"What is a bird dog, exactly?" I asked. "I mean, I've heard the word—only . . . well, I really don't know what it means."

Mr. Holdbrook smiled at me.

"They're dogs that are bred to hunt birds. Mostly quail or pheasant. What we have 'round here are bobwhite quail. They would much rather spend their time on the ground than flying 'round in the trees, like most birds. They're some of the best eating you ever stuck in your mouth." He stopped just long enough to lick his lips. "Bird dog smells where they been on the ground until he gets close enough to see 'em. What the birds do—remember, I told you they would rather spend their time on the ground— well, they covey up."

He must have noticed the confusion on my face.

"They bunch together in a clump. When they do that, the bird dog freezes, or points." He paused a moment. "Old Slim was a pointer. There's Brittany spaniels—kind of a short-range dog—they stay in real close to the hunter. German shorthair is kind of midrange. Pointer, like Slim, they love to run. You got to keep yellin' 'em back or they'll get plumb away from you." He smiled down at me. "Got to watch that with your—"

Suddenly he stopped, and shot a quick glance at Mama and Daddy. He cleared his throat.

"I mean, that's something *I* had to watch with Scooter. He liked to range pretty far away from me. Sure had to keep my eyes peeled. Never knew when them guys with the greyhounds might show up."

In that instant the sight of the pack of dogs attacking the coyote flashed through my mind. The memory sent a chill racing up my back. Before Mama or Daddy asked who Scooter was, Mr. Holdbrook started talking about Slim again. He told how, when they weren't hunting birds, he would sit in the old rocking chair and Slim would either curl up near his feet or climb up on his lap. "Old rascal was mite-near big as a horse." He chuckled. "Still thought he was a lapdog."

I loved listening to the old man. His voice was growly—almost mean sounding. And he didn't mince words or sugarcoat what he had to say. He just blurted stuff out. Guess when you're old, you can do that. But there was a gentleness to him. A tenderness in his eyes when he talked about his dog and hunting.

It was almost dark when Nathan and Mr. Holdbrook left. We walked them to the car. Before they drove away, he caught my eye and glanced at the pen. I knew he was reminding me to tell my parents.

I nodded.

"I will. Real soon."

Again, I thought about asking what he meant about the coyote being the best *and* the worst pet I would ever have. I never got the chance.

Chapter 15

Mr. Holdbrook was right. I needed to tell Mama and Daddy, and now was as good a time as any.

Trouble was, just as the Holdbrooks were driving down toward the road, another car came up. Adelee was coming home.

I needed to tell my folks before they found the pup. But I didn't want Adelee around when I did. It wouldn't hurt to wait awhile longer. It might be best to wait until I had the pup gentle enough so I could pet him. That way, it would be really hard for Mama and Daddy to say no. Soft, snuggly puppies are really hard to turn down.

I slipped off and trotted inside. I dialed Nolan and waited. It took forever for him to pick up.

"Nolan, this is Brad. Does your dad have welding gloves?"

There was a short silence.

"Hi, Brad. What?"

"Welding gloves. Do you know where he keeps them?"

"Yeah, they're out in the barn. Why?"

"Stick them in your backpack tomorrow," I told him. "Don't let your folks see you. Once we get to school, I'll take them. Got to go. Mama and Dad are coming. Bye."

I could hear Nolan saying something as I clicked the receiver back down. Voices came from the other room. Mama suggested someone take a seat on the couch, then asked if they'd like anything to drink. In a moment she came to the kitchen.

"We have guests," she said. "Would you please get a couple of glasses out of the cabinet and put ice in them for me?" She got the Coke bottle from the pantry.

I had to help her carry the Cokes in and get introduced to Jane Johnston and her mom and dad. We'd met them once or twice at a soccer game, but there's not much chance to visit while everybody's screaming and cheering. So we all sat around in the living room and talked.

After a while, Adelee and Jane asked if they could go out in the backyard and practice soccer. I got up and followed along.

It was almost too dark to see the ball, but they decided to play some, anyway. As usual, I got stuck in the middle of a keep-away game. The two girls would pass the ball and I had to try and get it away from them. I was really working hard, until I glanced out toward the barn.

The coyote stood there with his nose stuck through the fence. His little brown eyes followed the ball back and forth across our yard. Now and then, he'd pounce or shuffle his feet as if chasing it.

"Well, if you're not even going to try," Adelee snarled at me, "we might as well just quit."

Quickly, I spun back toward her, hoping she hadn't seen him.

"It's getting too dark to play, anyway," Jane said. She gave me a soft smile and followed Adelee to the back porch. My sister never glanced back.

Man. That was close.

They sat around and talked about soccer for

maybe two minutes, at the most, then they started talking about boys and how cute so-and-so was and how what's-his-name had a crush on what's-her-name, but how she didn't like him and on and on and on.

It was hard to decide which was more boring—Adelee's "boy" talk or the grown-ups talking about the weather or jobs and work in the living room. I went inside and played with Casey until everybody finally left.

Daddy went to the playroom to watch the news and Casey toddled off after him. Adelee asked Mama where her soccer uniform was and they headed to the washroom. I went to the fridge to see if I could find a snack.

It was a close call, out there in the backyard. I'd been lucky so far. If I could just keep him hidden for a couple more days, get him used to being picked up and petted, then Mama and Daddy would really like him. It would be so much fun to have a pet. They'd have to let me keep him and—

"BRADLEY JAMES McBRIDE!"

The way Mama screamed my name made me jump. She never used my whole name—not unless I was in deep trouble.

"BRADLEY! Get in here! NOW!"

Her voice sliced through the house like a knife. My teeth ground together inside my head as I trotted to find her.

"BRADLEY JAMES . . . I mean it! You get in here!"

Her voice came from the utility room.

She met me at the doorway. She had my red coat in one hand and Daddy's white shirt in the other.

Only my red coat wasn't red, and Daddy's white shirt wasn't white.

Adelee was sobbing and bawling like a little kid.

"My underwear . . . ," she moaned. "My socks . . . my soccer uniform . . ." She was blubbering now. "They're not white. They're . . . PINK!"

She glared up at me. If the hate in her eyes had been daggers, I would have been pinned to the wall and sliced into itsy-bitsy pieces.

Chapter 16

Okay—so how was I supposed to know that you don't soak bright colors in Clorox? Well—if it says "color-safe formula"—but not just regular, full-strength, plain old Clorox. And, okay—so how was I supposed to know that you don't wash colors in with the whites? I mean, shoot—I was only a kid.

Mama was mad. Adelee was so ticked off she was crying. Casey was bawling.

Daddy tried to come to my rescue—sort of.

"Come on, Adelee." He tried to soothe. "Nobody's going to see your underwear."

"But my uniform—" she broke off, whimpering.

Mama shook the shirt at him.

"How about your dress shirt?"

Daddy tried to smile.

"Well, I've got a lot of white shirts. Don't have any pink ones. I kind of like it—don't you?"

Mama shot him the same look she gave me. He clamped his lips together. Then, raising a hand to the corner of his mouth, he pretended to zip it shut. Daddy and Casey retreated to the playroom, leaving me to face Mama and Adelee alone.

Can't really say that I blamed him.

"Two weeks ain't all that bad," Nolan said, after we got to school Monday morning. He put a finger upside his nose and blew.

I jumped back. The other two guys who were standing with us jumped back and scattered, too.

Nolan wiped his nose and his chin, then flipped it on the ground.

"I've almost got it." He smiled.

Bill Preston and Neal LaForge looked at me and shook their heads. I sure wished Nolan would quit with that "farmer's blow" stuff.

Cautiously, we eased back together. Each of

us kept a watchful eye on Nolan—ready to dodge if he blew again.

"Yeah," Bill agreed. "Two weeks ain't bad at all. Last time I got grounded, it was for two whole *months.*"

"I got grounded for the rest of my life once," Neal added.

All three of us looked at him.

"How did you manage that?" I asked.

Neal grinned. "My sister had this jar of face cream. She'd been real snooty with me and I got fed up. You know how big sisters are."

Bill and I nodded. "And big brothers," Nolan added.

"Anyway," Neal went on, "I scooped all the face cream out of the jar and replaced it with this stuff called Icy Hot. Man . . ."—he gave a little chuckle—"you never heard so much squealing and screaming in your life. I thought she was gonna tear up the house."

The smile left his face. "It was funny—until my mom figured out what I'd done. Guess the face cream was expensive or something—"

He broke off, then patted me on the shoulder.

"Two weeks ain't bad. They'll forget after a little while."

I shook my head and unzipped my backpack. The three guys watched while I pulled out my *pink* coat. "As long as it's cold, they won't forget."

Nolan giggled. Bill slapped a hand over his mouth. Neal sighed. "Okay—so you're grounded for two weeks. It usually starts warming up around the second week in April. When you don't need that coat anymore, they'll forget."

I couldn't help notice a little twinkle in Neal's eye. "It's a really cute coat, though. Never saw a guy in a pink coat before."

It was bad enough to be grounded for two weeks. I couldn't go anyplace with my friends, I couldn't watch TV or mess with my PlayStation. I had to go straight to my room after supper and do homework—whether I had any homework or not. All that was bad enough.

What was worse was when I went to gym class. Coach Landon always walked through the locker room when we changed out of our school stuff and into our shorts and gym shoes.

"Cute socks," he said. Then he walked on.

All the guys around heard him. They looked at my pink socks and elbowed one another. It wasn't too bad.

But I still had to get my jeans off and my gym shorts on. I tried to change quickly so no one would notice.

It didn't work.

When Dad came to my room that afternoon, I told him all about it. He gave me a hug.

"Don't take it so hard, Brad. They were just teasing. I mean, if they pester you all the time, you could be a nerd or something. But this type of teasing over something like that . . . well, guys usually don't tease unless they really like you. You know—unless you're popular."

"I'm popular, all right." I had to bite down on my bottom lip to keep from sniffling. "Everybody in school knows who I am . . ." I broke off, unable to finish.

"It was horrible, Dad. They started saying things like 'Look at those pretty pink *panties*,' and . . . and all sorts of stuff."

"I'm sorry, Brad." Daddy hugged me again. "Just try not to let them get to you."

"But it was horrible."

"I know. I know." He sighed. "What a rotten way to spend your birthday."

My eyes sprang open.

Today *was* my birthday!

I had been so busy thinking about the coyote pup and the laundry and getting grounded and the guys making fun of me at school . . . well, I completely forgot about my birthday.

When Daddy reminded me, I almost smiled. *Almost.* The smile never quite made it to my face, because I remembered what a rotten day it had been.

Dad nudged me with his elbow. "I think I've got something that might make you feel better." He stood up and motioned me to follow him. "Come on. It's outside."

Chapter 17

Mama was working in the kitchen. When Daddy and I walked through the living room, she peeked around the corner.

"You're still grounded," she snapped. "Just where do you think you're going?"

My mouth opened, but nothing came out.

"I need help with something outside," Daddy called. Quickly he put a finger to his lips, telling me to stay quiet. "Brad's going to help me with it."

He shushed me again. I waited, frozen in my tracks, until Mama disappeared back into the kitchen. At the end of the driveway, Daddy turned to me and smiled.

"Look, Brad. Your mother doesn't know about this, yet. It'd probably be a good idea to keep it quiet for a couple of days. You know, until she cools off about the washing machine thing. But you've wanted this for a long time. And . . . well . . ." He put his arm around me as we walked toward the barn. "You're old enough to take the responsibility."

The breath caught in my throat. It must be a bicycle. I'd been asking for a new one ever since we moved here. One with wide, cross-country tires so I could ride it on the gravel roads and through the pasture. I could hardly wait.

"I'd put it off," Daddy confessed, "until Mr. Holdbrook showed up the other day. Listening to him talk and watching your eyes light up . . . well . . . like I said. I think it's about time."

That threw me. Mr. Holdbrook hadn't mentioned anything about a bicycle—had he?

Daddy stopped at the gate to the coyote pen.

A lump came up in my throat.

Daddy had seen the coyote. He was going to kill me. No. He was too happy. He didn't want to tell Mama. That meant he was going to let me keep him! No . . . that wasn't it, either.

Daddy frowned. "He was here a second ago. I just put him in there. Where could he—"

All of a sudden, there was a loud squealing sound. It was followed by some clunking and rattling around inside the dome-shaped doghouse. Then there was more squealing.

A white streak flew from the opening. Right on its heels was a brown streak. The streaks made two laps around the pen, then stopped at the far corner.

"What is it?" I asked, pointing at a white creature with a long, pointed tail and floppy ears.

"It's a bird dog pup," Daddy answered. "You've been wanting a pet. Mr. Holdbrook got to talking about his bird dog and your face lit up and . . . and . . . What is *that?*" He pointed.

I swallowed the lump in my throat. "It's a coyote pup. I caught him the day before Mr. Holdbrook came. The other coyotes were all dead and I knew he wouldn't make it. I . . . I was going to tell you and Mama. Honest! I just wanted to get him gentle, first, and . . . and . . ."

The bird dog was mostly white, with a blotch of orange on one ear and another at the base of his tail. He was bigger than my pup, but he cow-ered while the coyote bared his teeth and snarled at him.

A ridge of hair raised up on the coyote's back. The bird dog fell over on his side and wagged his tail. When he did that, the coyote quit snarling, but his hair still stuck up.

The bird dog wagged his tail, wiggled, and flopped around. Then he got real still and didn't move a muscle. Cautiously, the coyote leaned forward and sniffed him. Then the white pup struggled to his feet and sniffed back, keeping himself lower than the coyote. He wagged his tail so hard that his rear end waved back and forth. The ridge on the coyote's back began to flatten.

I smiled when I noticed that both their tails were wagging.

"You think they like each other?"

Daddy shrugged.

"I don't know."

We had been watching the two animals so intently that neither of us had looked at the other. Then I felt Daddy's eyes on me. He wasn't smiling.

"You know you can't keep him, don't you, Brad?"

"Why not? If they get along together and don't try to hurt each other . . ."

Daddy shook his head.

"It's a wild animal. You can't tame something as wild as a coyote. You need to—"

"Yes I can," I interrupted. "Mr. Holdbrook had two coyotes for pets. One was named Doofus and the other Scooter. He said that Doofus never did gentle down and he had to let him go. But he said that Scooter was the best pet he ever had."

We both turned our attention back to the pups. They were chasing each other around the pen.

It was really fun to watch. They were quick and agile, but they were puppies, too, kind of clumsy sometimes. They'd run and dodge, then one would trip over his own feet and the other would slam into the back of him. Both would go rolling. Then they'd chase the other way until the one in front tripped and they went tumbling over and over. At times, all I could see was a tangle of long, clumsy legs and two tails and dust.

The thing I enjoyed the most was the smile on Daddy's face.

The smile stayed there until their chase game got too close to where we were standing. All of a sudden, the coyote looked up at us and shot back to his doghouse, like the devil himself was chasing him.

Daddy looked at me. "I thought you said he was gentle."

I shook my head. "No. Not yet. I was waiting until I got him gentle before I told you about him, remember?"

I explained what Mr. Holdbrook had said.

Daddy didn't much like the sound of it, but he agreed to let me try.

"But not now!" He glanced toward the house. "Your mother and Adelee are making you a birthday cake. Act surprised, okay?"

I nodded. Daddy was still staring at the house. He heaved a heavy sigh. The little bird dog pup came over to us. He was about to shake himself apart, wagging his tail and wiggling all over. Daddy looked back at me.

Finally he took one more look toward the house and nodded.

"That woman . . ."

(I noticed how he didn't say, "Your mom" or "My wife" or even "Rhonda." He just said, "That woman.")

"That woman is going to kill us."

Chapter 18

The second we got back to the house, I shot to my bedroom and got busy on homework. I managed to finish almost everything before Mama called me for supper.

I was so happy about my pups, I could hardly stand it. Still, I tried to look really sorry for myself when I walked through the house.

I'd barely stepped into the kitchen when everyone shouted: "Happy Birthday!" My eyes flashed wide and I took a big step back. They sang "Happy Birthday" to me and had me blow out the candles. I got them all in one breath.

Adelee gave me a new CD for my PlayStation. It was a good one. I didn't even think that Adelee knew about stuff like that. Casey gave me a new sweater. (Well, Mama picked it out.)

Mama and Dad gave me a couple of shirts and a new pair of jeans.

We had supper, then ate cake and ice cream until I was about to pop.

Daddy excused himself and headed for the front door.

"I thought we were *all* going out there," Mama called.

Daddy froze. "I think I'll put it on the front porch, instead."

Mama looked a little confused. She took a load of dishes to the sink. When she came back, she told Adelee to come with her. I started to get up.

"Just Adelee," Mama said. "Wait here until we call you." She picked Casey up in one arm and got the camera with her free hand. "Wait," she repeated.

I didn't have to wait for very long. When they called, I trotted through the living room and out onto the porch.

It was probably the neatest birthday I ever had. The new bicycle was GREAT! It was a mountain bike, with big, heavy tires and low-range gears for climbing. It was a lot sturdier than my old bicycle.

Since it was my birthday, Mama said I could ride it. "You're still grounded," she cautioned. "Fifteen minutes each day, after you get home from school. Then straight to your room and homework."

"Yes, ma'am."

The bicycle was great. The clothes were okay. The new puppy was FANTABULOUS! But the best thing of all was Daddy. It was like the two of us were really together—maybe against the whole world. Just the two of us. I don't really know how to explain it, but it made me feel really special.

Mama was serious about being grounded. She set the timer on the stove for exactly fifteen minutes. Daddy went in to help her with the dishes. I went flying down the road on my bike. Near the bottom, I shifted to the lowest gear, turned around and rode back up. The thing was unbelievable. It wasn't even like I was pedaling up hill. Fifteen minutes seemed as quick as the blink of an eye. I parked my bike beside the rocking chair.

"Don't go in yet!" Daddy called. He yelled a lot louder than he needed to. "I want some help moving the rest of that stuff. As soon as it gets dark you can go in and do your homework."

When I followed him past the kitchen window, I knew why he had been so loud. Mama was still doing the dishes. He stopped at his car, pushed down on the trunk, and turned the key—really slow. Then, trying not to make a sound, he lifted the trunk. There was a sack of puppy food. I got it out. Daddy pushed the trunk down, slow and easy with both hands. He leaned on it until it made a faint clicking sound.

I led the way to the hay silo. Daddy followed. I showed him the food that Nolan had sneaked over. He stood there and shook his head.

Daddy opened the can while I went after the bowl. The little bird dog was all over me from the second I opened the gate. He jumped against my leg and wagged his tail and wiggled all over. When I reached down to pet him, he licked my hand.

Daddy looked at the directions on the puppy food bag. "You didn't bring a measuring cup, did you?"

I shook my head.

He squinted at the directions. "It says about a cup. But since we're feeding two of them, we can double it. We'll just have to guess."

He poured the dry food in and I dumped the canned meat on top. Daddy stirred it up real good with the knife. There was no way I could get past the bird dog—not carrying the bowl of food. The puppy went totally bonkers.

He wiggled and waggled and tried to get me to pick him up or play with him. He was just too cute to resist. I handed Daddy the bowl and swooped him up in my arms.

Holding that puppy was like trying to hold a handful of worms. I didn't know anything could squirm and twist and flop and wiggle that much. His little legs were going every which direction and he was twisting and turning and . . .

I finally hugged him against me, which kept him from wiggling out of my arms. But it also put his long, pink tongue in range of my face. Before I could latch the gate, I felt like I'd had a bath.

I had petted Bowzer, but he just lay there.

This puppy loved to be picked up and hugged. It was like being close to me was the neatest thing in the world. I couldn't keep from giggling. Daddy chuckled, too, just watching us.

I finally set the puppy down and Daddy handed me the food bowl. I put it in front of the doghouse and stepped back. The puppy looked at me, like he wanted to play some. Then he sniffed the food. Then he looked at me again.

The food finally won. I smiled when he started gobbling his meal.

When I look back on it—I should have known better. Even though the coyote was really scared of me, when there was food around he wasn't scared at all.

He came flying out of his doghouse and landed smack-dab in the middle of the bowl. Only this time, someone else was there, eating *his* food.

The squealing and yelping was enough to wake the dead. Growling and snarling, he was all over the bird dog. I rushed in to rescue the pup. He was whimpering and whining like he was half dead. Only when I looked him over, he wasn't bleeding. In fact, there wasn't a mark on him. He was just scared.

I snuggled him against me. Then, like he forgot all about the whole thing, he started wagging and wiggling and licking me in the face.

"Is he okay?" Daddy asked.

I handed him over the fence. "I think so. Guess he was just scared."

Daddy petted him. He laughed when the puppy licked him all over. The coyote stood, surrounding his food with his paws, and glared. Latching the gate behind me, I joined Daddy.

"He's not hurt." Daddy smiled. He wiped his wet chin with his shirtsleeve. The instant he did, the puppy licked him again. "He's fine. You'd think he was being killed. Tomorrow—"

Daddy never finished what he was saying. His eyes suddenly flashed wide. Ever so slowly, I turned to see what he was looking at.

Mama stood beside the barn. Her arms were folded and she patted one foot. She patted it so hard, dust puffed up from the gravel. Daddy made a gulping sound.

"Uh-oh!"

Chapter 19

I didn't know daddies could get grounded. I thought kids were the only ones who got grounded.

Daddy said he *wasn't* grounded. He said Mama was just a little upset.

Mama said she wasn't mad because he bought me a puppy. She said she wasn't mad because I rescued a baby coyote. She was mad because neither of us had the decency to tell her.

Casey didn't say anything.

Adelee said that *Brat* didn't need a dog or a coyote, either one. She said that *Brat* never did anything and *Brat* wouldn't take care of them and they'd either starve to death or Mama would end up having to feed them. She was so snotty.

I couldn't help myself. I stuck my tongue out at her.

Dumb move.

"Okay, so you're grounded for a month." Nolan shrugged. "No big deal. It's only two weeks longer than before. Besides, now you don't have to go sneaking around anymore."

"I know." I leaned against the flag pole. "But . . . well . . . sneaking around was kind of fun. Especially when Daddy was with me . . . just the two of us having a secret and . . ."

Nolan put his finger up to the side of his nose. Neal, Bill, and I scattered.

"That's really gross," Bill complained when we all gathered back around the flagpole.

"No kiddin'," Neal agreed. Then he turned to me. "So when can we see the coyote? Are you gonna like bring him to school, or maybe we could come out to your house?"

My shoulders sagged. "I'm grounded. Remember?"

The bell sounded about the time Nolan was getting ready to blow again. The three of us darted away from him and toward the building. We didn't even bother to look back.

I liked school. The only part I dreaded was gym class. I was good in gym. I wasn't the world's greatest athlete, but I wasn't too bad, either. What I dreaded most was the locker room.

I mean, running around in pink underwear was *not* cool.

The pink underwear faded after a while. So did being grounded.

Daddy wasn't grounded nearly as long as I was. He and Mama had a "discussion." (Mama and Daddy didn't have fights, they had "discussions.") Only this discussion was loud enough that it worried Adelee and me. Casey woke up crying, so it didn't last very long.

Anyway, Daddy was ungrounded after two nights. I got ungrounded after two and a half weeks.

A lot happened during those two and a half weeks, though.

* * *

I named my coyote Scooter—after Mr. Holdbrook's. Daddy gave me a pair of thick leather gloves, which I wore under Mr. Bigbee's welding gloves. Scooter snarled and snapped and tried his best to tear me up. It hurt—even through the gloves. But he didn't tear them up or break my skin.

After three or four attempts, I could pick him up without gloves. He would wiggle and squirm and try to lick me in the face—just like my new dog.

On Wednesday of the second week I was grounded, Daddy and I took the bird dog and the coyote to get their puppy shots. Doctor Traylor was really nice. He made over Scooter so much that the little coyote was almost turning flips. Scooter didn't even notice when he gave him his rabies shot. But the bird dog pup didn't care if he was gentle or not—he growled when he took his temperature. (Can't say I blamed him. I'd probably growl if someone tried to take my temperature that way, too.)

We named the bird dog Button. That's because he started chewing on the TV remote, the first time we let him in the house. Daddy didn't notice him. His sharp little teeth were hitting the buttons like mad and the TV kept switching channels and getting louder, then softer. Daddy thought the TV was getting ready to blow up or something. He grabbed Casey and headed for the other room. While he was leaving, he saw the pup chewing the remote.

The first time I sneaked him into my bedroom, Button got hold of the joystick on my PlayStation and did the same thing. I had the sound off so Mama wouldn't know I was playing with it, and he almost got me caught.

There was another big fight over the food bowl. Even though Scooter was becoming gentle and easy to handle, when it came to food, he didn't change one bit. I learned never to leave my hand near the bowl after putting it on the ground. And when it came to sharing with Button—*forget it!*

Daddy bought another bowl, so they wouldn't fight. But Scooter thought both bowls belonged to him. Anyway, we were afraid to leave Button and Scooter together in the same pen. We put Button and his food in the backyard. He really liked it there because he was close to us. My bird dog loved people. Daddy went out and petted him. Adelee even went out a couple of times. I could hear her laughing, clear back in my bedroom. Mama played with him, too, although she pretended she didn't want anything to do with him. Button loved it . . .

Until it got dark.

I always slept with my window opened. Even in the dead of winter, I kept it up just a crack, because I liked the fresh air and nestling down in all the covers. I was almost asleep when I heard this weird whining sound. Rolling over and wrapping the pillow around my head didn't make it stop.

Finally, I got up and peeked out the window. Button was standing in the middle of our backyard. He lay down and whimpered. Then he leaped to his feet and turned around—real quick—like something was sneaking up on him. When he didn't see anything, he lay down again, only to whine and jump up to look the other way.

"What's wrong, pup?" I asked in a soft voice. "You scared?"

The instant he heard me, Button made a beeline straight to my window. He stretched his paws up as far as he could reach and started bouncing up and down and whining. He kept getting louder and louder, and I just knew he was going to wake Mama and Daddy and Casey. There was only one thing to do.

I opened the screen, leaned out, and picked him up. He squirmed and wiggled and licked me in the face. I plopped him down on the bed.

Even in the dark, he wanted to play. He kept trying to slurp me with his long tongue. When I held him down, he started chewing on my hand. His teeth were really sharp. He wagged his tail so hard, it thumped on the bedspread like a drum.

The only way I could keep him still was to take hold of the back of his neck and shove him down hard. It took about ten times before he finally got the idea that he was supposed to go to sleep. Even then, every time I felt him try to get up, I had to clunk him again.

After a couple of nights, when I'd open the window and pick him up, he'd flop down next to me on the bed and curl up in the crook of my leg. A few times, he'd need to go to the bathroom. I'd unlatch the screen and drop him. Soon as he finished, he'd come flying right back to my window and jump up and down until I lifted him inside.

Sleeping with my bird dog was fun. It was kind of neat to feel him snuggle down into the crook of my leg. It made him feel warm and safe. It made me feel safe, too.

Sleeping with my bird dog AND my coyote . . . that was another matter.

Chapter 20

"Mr. McBride!"

The loud, sudden voice startled me. I'd had my elbows resting on my desk with my fists against my cheeks holding up my head. I guess I'd fallen asleep. I jerked and my elbows slipped. When they did, my forehead bumped the desk.

Everybody in class was laughing at me. Mrs. Holt stood above me with her arms folded. She wasn't the least bit amused.

"Brad, that makes twice this week that you've fallen asleep in library class. Just because there's only two weeks of school left, it's no excuse." She stopped talking long enough to turn and shoot the rest of the class a dirty look. When they quit laughing, she turned back to me. "This isn't like you. Is there something going on at home?"

"No, ma'am. I just haven't been sleeping too well the last couple of nights."

"Is there something bothering you?" She frowned.

I shook my head. "No . . . not that I can think of."

She sighed.

"This is library time, not nap time. If it happens again, I'll have to tell your mother about it when she gets back to school. You understand?"

"Yes, ma'am. It won't happen again."

Things had gone pretty well until Casey came down with the chicken pox. Chicken pox had been no big deal. Catching chicken pox is just something little kids do. Adelee and I had both had them, when we were little. But the problem came when Mama stayed home to take care of Casey.

That very first day, Mama had met Daddy and me at the door, the second we got in from school.

"We've got a problem," she'd announced. She shushed us and led the way to the back door. There, she pointed out into the yard.

Button was racing up and down the fence, yapping his fool head off. Scooter was running up and down the fence in *his* pen, barking back at Button.

"This has been going on all day," Mama sighed. "When they're not barking at each other, Button lays down near the back door and whines. They miss each other."

So . . .

We kept them in separate pens to feed them. After they finished eating, I brought Scooter into the backyard.

The pups would run and play and wrestle and chase. It was fun to watch them. Button would chase Scooter. They'd run in a big circle, out around the pine tree in the far corner of the yard and disappear at the side of the house. Then here would come Button with Scooter chasing him. Back and forth, round and round—neither of them ever seemed to run out of energy.

Even when it got dark.

That first night, I thought about leaving them both outside. But Button started jumping against my window and whining. As soon as I picked him up and plopped him on my bed, here came Scooter. I latched the screen and tried to ignore him. He just jumped higher and whined louder. I opened the screen and picked him up.

The second his little paws touched the bed, he and Button would go at each other. They start biting and growling and play fighting. One night I grabbed Button by the scruff of the neck with one hand and Scooter with the other. Then, I lifted both of them off the bed and held them in front of me so I could glare at them.

"Look you two, we can't keep doing this," I growled at them in my loudest whisper. (It's hard to growl and whisper at the same time, but if I said it any louder, my parents might hear.) "I can't get any sleep with you two wrestling and playing all night. I got in trouble at school today, for sleeping in class. So tonight, things are going to be different. You'll have to play during the day. At night we're all three going to go to sleep. Got it?"

Even dangling in midair, they were both still trying to paw each other.

"Okay. If you're not going to listen—we'll do it the hard way."

With that, I shoved Button down as hard as I could into the mattress. When he tried to hop up, I shoved him again. I did the same with Scooter. It took some pushing, but finally both of them settled down. Slowly, I let go of them and nestled my head into the pillow. My pups lay still for a moment, then Scooter eased up on his feet.

Before he could hop across me and start playing with Button, I took hold of the corner of my pillow. Raising my head, I quickly lifted the pillow and brought it down on top of the coyote. There was a little whoomp, followed by a squeak.

"Lay down!" I ordered.

With my free hand, I pushed Button. He stayed put, but after a minute, Scooter tried to get up a second time. I whopped him again with the pillow. After I thumped him about four or five times, Scooter finally got the idea.

If I lay on my back, with one hand on Button and the other on Scooter, it seemed to calm them. Button had the softest little ears—they were like velvet or silk. They weren't really little either—they were kind of big and floppy. They didn't stick up like Scooter's ears did, but I loved rubbing them or feeling them between my fingers and thumb.

If I let go of Scooter, he would nudge me with his nose. His nose was always wet and cold as ice. He would keep nudging until I put my hand on him and petted him.

Sleeping flat on my back, with a hand on each of my pups, took some getting used to. But I managed to get plenty of sleep those last two weeks of school and didn't get in trouble for nodding off in class.

The whole family found out about the two pups sleeping in my bed, the first week after school was out. I liked the way summer vacation worked in Oklahoma a lot better than in Chicago. There, it seemed like we went to school until the middle of summer. Here, we got out the second week of May.

Oklahoma has weird weather in May. We had a big rainstorm one night. I was sleeping so soundly, it didn't wake me. I might have slept right through it, if Daddy hadn't come in to close my window. The first thing I knew, Daddy was crashing around my room, yelling bad words in the dark. Scooter was growling and Button was sitting on my chest with his tail pushed against my face, yapping his fool head off.

I shoved him away and sat up, just about the time Mama came racing in and turned on the light.

Daddy stood in the corner of my room. A bunch of CDs and some books were scattered on the floor around him.

As soon as I sat up, Button hopped off my chest and scampered to hide behind me. He peeked around my side, yapping as loud as he could.

"What in the world . . ." Mama gasped.

"The window . . . trying to close it . . . keep the rain out . . ." Daddy kept stammering instead of talking. "Leaned across the bed . . . something attacked me . . ."

Suddenly Button recognized Mama and Daddy. He hushed his barking and leaned against me. Scooter was no place in sight. Daddy glanced down. Then he shoved his way out of the corner and walked over to me.

He cleared his throat. Then he lifted his right arm.

Scooter dangled from the sleeve of Daddy's pajamas. He snarled and shook his head back and forth. Only since he was hanging in midair, when he shook his head, all of him flopped around. Even his tail spun.

Daddy scowled down at me.

"You mind getting your coyote off my arm?"

Chapter 21

It's a wonder us kids ever get to be grown-ups.

I mean, between all the falling we do when we're little like Casey, trying to get across a street without getting run down, the falling out of trees and wrecking bicycles—it's amazing that any of us even live to be thirteen. Along with all that, there's getting in trouble with our parents.

I expected Mama and Daddy to kill me.

They didn't.

In fact, once things settled down and they realized that no one was seriously hurt, they didn't even yell at me.

When Daddy stuck his arm out, I grabbed Scooter. He was latched on to that sleeve like his life depended on it. When I got hold of him, he let go. After I put him on my bed, his little ears pressed down against his head, and he flattened himself—like he was embarrassed. Then he slinked around to hide with Button.

Daddy was tall and slender, but he did have a little roll around his middle. He called it his spare tire. (Mama called it something else, only I don't remember what.) After we got Scooter off his arm, he raised his pajama top to look at his spare tire. There were two sets of teeth marks where Scooter had bitten him. The spots were red, but they weren't bleeding. We got lucky with his arm, too. There were a couple of scratches, but mostly Scooter had hold of the sleeve and, aside from ripping some holes there, he didn't do all that much damage.

Daddy sat on the foot of my bed. Mama stood beside him, inspecting his wounds. Adelee was at my doorway with Casey in her arms.

"It was dark," Daddy said, trying to laugh it off. "Guess he didn't recognize me and thought somebody was trying to get Brad. He was just protecting his boy. Darndest thing I ever saw. I mean, he was after me! He was going to keep me away from Brad, no matter what."

Mama didn't see any humor in it at all. But she wasn't so mad at Scooter that she made me throw him outside.

Adelee just curled her nose. "*Brat's* probably got fleas," she muttered. Then she went to put Casey back in bed.

Daddy, Mama, and I talked for a little while. I assured them that Scooter and Button didn't have fleas. They were put out that I had sneaked the pups into bed. But they decided it wasn't such a bad idea to let me keep them inside—at least at night. "That coyote is better than a burglar alarm." Daddy chuckled.

I was glad they let me keep the pups in my room. I really liked having them to snuggle with at night.

Even Adelee came around to my pups, about the second week of vacation. Summer Soccer League started as soon as school was out, but they didn't have any games until the middle of June. She really wanted to make varsity soccer at school next year, so every afternoon she made me practice with her.

I griped about it some, but I really didn't mind, because Nolan was busy helping his dad with the wheat harvest. When they finished, about the third week in June, we could go fishing or ride our bikes and stuff. But with him working all the time, there wasn't anybody to play with. Practicing soccer with Adelee was about it.

Early each morning, I fed Scooter and Button. I fixed Scooter's food bowl in the house. I'd learned right off that Scooter *wanted his food.* If I held the bowl down at my side, he'd jump up and try to get it. One time, he almost got my hand. So, once I was outside, I held it high above my head.

Scooter followed me out to his pen. The tricky part was keeping him outside when I slipped through the gate. It really improved my soccer skills, I guess. I mean, I didn't kick him, but I had to use my foot to shove him aside and dart in before he made it through the gate. Once I had the food on the ground, I opened the pen and got out of his way. Then I went back and fed Button. Scooter always finished first. He'd put his front feet in his bowl and growl—telling the whole world that this was *his food* and he wasn't going to share.

Button was a lot calmer. He just wagged his tail and wiggled all over. He'd much rather be petted than eat.

When Button finished, I picked up his bowl and took it inside. Then I let Scooter out of his pen to come and play in the backyard. They wrestled and chased and raced around until they were tired. Then Button would sniff the edge of the fence for birds, or stare up in the trees. Scooter usually took a nap.

The first afternoon Adelee dragged me out to practice with her, Scooter was asleep on the back porch. We went out in the middle of the yard and started passing the ball back and forth. After we were loosened up a little, Adelee tried to dribble the ball from one fence to the other. I was supposed to get it away from her. Then I had to dribble it so she could try to steal it from me.

Adelee had just started her second run when we heard growling and snarling. Both of us froze in our tracks. Before we focused, a brown streak came flying from the back porch and pounced onto the soccer ball. We jumped back.

Scooter attacked the ball.

When he pounced, he landed on top of it. It rolled. He ended up turning a somersault and landing flat on his back. That didn't faze him, though. He scrambled to his feet and went after the ball again.

He growled and snarled and snapped. Thing was, it was pretty big around and Scooter was still kind of small. He couldn't get his teeth into the ball. So every time he hit it with his mouth, it rolled.

Adelee and I stood like dummies, with our mouths open, as the little coyote chased the ball all around the yard.

"He's going to bust it," Adelee complained.

I just smiled and shook my head.

"No. He can't get his teeth in it."

She folded her arms. "Well, go get it. We can't practice if he's got the ball."

I strolled over to where Scooter had the ball against the chain-link fence. Cautiously, I eased my foot down next to the ball and scooped it away from him. He charged after it and started herding it across the yard once more. He used his front paws to try and guide it, and his mouth and snout to shove it along.

When I caught up to him the second time and kicked it away, I quickly put myself between him and the ball. For just an instant, I thought to myself—Man, that's really dumb, Brad. He's going to chew your leg off. But that thought only lasted an instant. Scooter came flying around to the side and tried to get it again. I trapped it and held it with my foot. He growled and sounded vicious as could be. Only, all the time he was growling and sounding ugly, his bushy tail was waving back and forth like a flag in a strong breeze. He was careful not to hit my leg or foot with his teeth.

I did a spin-turn and quickly kicked the ball across the yard to Adelee. Scooter took off after it. When Adelee saw him coming, she didn't even try to dribble it away from him. Her eyes got as big as the ball, and she booted it back to me.

Only Scooter intercepted.

I thought it was funny. Both of us were amazed at how quick he was. Adelee was still a little irritated, until . . .

While I was going after the ball, Mama opened the back door and stuck her head out.

"He's pretty good at that," she called. "He's not biting you, is he?"

"No, ma'am. He's talking trash, but he just goes for the ball."

She laughed. "You two get where you can dribble and pass the ball without that coyote stealing it—you'll both be good enough to make the varsity team."

Adelee's face lit up. From that moment on, we never practiced soccer without the coyote.

Chapter 22

Scooter improved at soccer a lot quicker than Adelee and I did. Course he cheated, too. We could only kick with one foot at a time. Scooter used both front paws, his mouth, nose, and his forehead. Having four legs, instead of two, he was a lot quicker than Adelee and me as well.

It took both of us, dribbling and passing the ball back and forth, to get it from one end of the yard to the other. Even at that, about half the time Scooter managed to steal it. Jane Johnston came to spend the night with Adelee, and as soon as Scooter and Button finished eating the next morning, we dragged her out to practice.

She couldn't believe her eyes. "He's awesome!" she said. She said it over and over and over.

One against three was pretty fair. Still, if we didn't watch our passes or got sloppy with them, Scooter was right there and managed to take the ball away.

Button couldn't have cared less about soccer. He totally ignored us and stayed out of the way while we were practicing. He sniffed around trees or barked at birds fluttering about.

When we took a break, Button would show up. He'd wiggle, trying to get somebody to pet him, or he'd put his paws up and try to get us to lift him on our laps. If we didn't pay any attention, he'd sit down on my foot. Why he liked to sit on my foot, I had no idea.

During the summer, the principals and the custodians were the only ones at school. One day Daddy mentioned something to one of the maintenance men about how my bird dog barked at birds. This guy told him that bird dogs weren't supposed to bark; they were supposed to *point* at birds with their nose. Since neither of us knew the first thing about training a bird dog, Daddy called a trainer—the guy he bought Button from.

Daddy talked, and I listened on the portable phone in the playroom.

"Nothing to worry about," Mr. Wilson said. "He's still a puppy. What you need to do now, is obedience work."

"What's that?" I asked.

There was a second or two of silence on the phone.

"That's my son Brad."

"Oh, hi, Brad," Mr. Wilson said. "Your pup's a good one. You enjoying him, so far?"

I smiled. "Yes, sir!"

"Just keep playing with him and having fun," Mr. Wilson said. "As far as training, the only thing you need to do right now, is get him so he'll come when you call his name or whistle."

"How do I do that?"

"Ah . . ." Mr. Wilson paused for a moment. "Well, a lot of people put doggie treats in their pockets. Don't use candy, but wieners or doggie treats—something like that. Whenever he comes to you, give him a reward.

"Some dogs don't care much for food. Just pet them and praise them whenever they come.

Some dogs . . . well, some are a little hard-headed. Don't like treats and couldn't care less if you praise them. If your pup is one of those . . . about the only thing you can do is run him down."

"Huh?"

"Call him and if he won't come, chase him down. Talk real mean and act like you're gonna eat him up. Then drag him back where you want him to be. Once he's there, you can pet him and tell him what a good dog he is."

I'm glad Adelee had me in pretty good shape from practicing soccer with her. I never did so much running in my life as when I was trying to catch Button.

With Scooter all I had to do was stick my hand in my pocket, like I was digging for a treat, and call his name. The big challenge was not losing a finger.

Button couldn't care less about treats. He liked being petted and loved on *unless* there was some interesting smell in the grass. When that happened, his head went down, and his nose worked so hard that it made a little popping sound. And, as far as getting him to come, I could yell his name or whistle until I was blue in the face, and he never so much as looked up.

Part of the problem was my whistling. It wasn't all that loud. So Mama loaned me the playground whistle she used at school.

The pups and I spent most of the time on our eighty acres behind the house. There were a few hills, a little canyon, and a creek back there—lots of places to roam and explore.

And that's what we did, almost every day.

I missed my friends at school. And it seemed like, instead of four weeks, it had been a couple of months since I'd seen Nolan. He'd called last Tuesday and said it would be another week or two before he could get loose to go fishing. I could hardly wait.

But while I was waiting, I sure had fun with my pups.

One morning, I got up real early. I guess the thought of taking my bike had been hanging around in my head for a while and I just didn't know it. But it was there, plain as day, when I woke up. It would be a lot faster to run down

Button. I got my bike and went to open the back gate. Scooter shot out first, but Button was hot on his heels. I got on my bike, blew the playground whistle, and headed up the hill behind the house.

The bicycle worked great as long as we stayed on the gravel road. But when Button stuck his nose to the ground and started chasing a smell out across the pasture . . .

I blew the whistle. He ignored me. I whipped the handlebars to the side and took after him. I was gaining on him pretty quick. In fact, a lot faster than I usually did on foot. Until I came to this little ravine.

It was small and I didn't see it in the tall grass, until a split second before I hit it. There was nothing I could do.

One second, I was intent on my pup—blowing the whistle and calling his name. The next, I was flat on my face in the dirt, picking grass out of my teeth.

Before I could get up, Button and Scooter came racing over, wagging their tails and licking me in the face. They liked having me down on the ground with them—down on their level—

because they were all over me. When I finally managed to get up and look myself over, the damage wasn't too bad. I had grass stains on my right knee and a scratch on my right elbow. But I'd gotten scraped up worse than this playing soccer with Adelee. My bicycle was a little worse off than I was.

The wheel wasn't bent and the tire was still full of air, but the handlebars were pointed the wrong way.

I got hold of them and straddled the front tire. Even straining and shoving as hard as I could, I couldn't twist them back in line. So I walked the bike back to the house.

Daddy was sitting in the rocking chair, drinking his coffee, when I got there. He found his wrench set and loosened the nut on the handlebars. When we had everything lined up just right, he tightened it down for me.

"Might ride on the road," he suggested. "Safer than cross-country."

I smiled at him and shook my head.

"There aren't many cars, but until those pups come the second I yell . . . you know, out on the road . . . with a car coming."

Daddy's eyebrows arched up. "Yeah, know what you mean." He thought a moment. "How about the alfalfa field?"

"Great idea, Daddy."

Why it didn't occur to me that it was Saturday, I'll never know.

Chapter 23

Nolan's dad had already harvested the wheat from the field in front of our place. As soon as they were done, they brought in two tractors and plowed the short stalks that were left. The dirt now looked smooth and soft.

Beyond the wheat field was the alfalfa field and then Tony Hollow Creek. Once I got to the alfalfa or the cow paths on the side of the creeks, I could ride forever.

The hill down to the road was steep and I coasted most of the way. Yelling at Button and Scooter kept them beside me until we crossed the road. At the edge of the field, they squeezed under the barbed wire and took off. Now that they were safe and away from any cars that might come along, I breathed a little easier.

But by the time I got my bicycle to the alfalfa field, I was hardly breathing at all.

I never realized trail bikes were so heavy. First off was the fence. Straining and pushing and shoving, I finally gave up on trying to lift the bike over the barbed wire and decided it would be easier to slide it under. Even at that, I had to pull up the bottom strand of wire with one hand while dragging the heavy bicycle under with the other.

And if that wasn't hard enough, next was the plowed field.

The dirt was red, smooth, and pretty as could be. It was also soft as warm butter. Each time I hopped on my bike, the tires sank. Finally, realizing there was no way I was going to ride the thing, I decided to walk it.

By the time I got through the second barbed wire fence and into the alfalfa, I was exhausted. Water dripped from my hair down the back of my neck. From the house the alfalfa field looked smooth, but it was full of ruts and gopher mounds.

When I finally dragged my bicycle under the last fence, I collapsed.

I don't know how long I stayed, cooling off and enjoying the rest. It wasn't as long as I wanted or needed. The thing was, I peeked up and realized both pups were gone. Struggling to my knees, I blew the whistle. There was still no sign of them—not even Scooter. I whistled again.

Suddenly, Button appeared on the far side of the pond. He didn't really appear—it was more like I saw this white streak go flying through the grass. I blew the whistle again. He didn't even look up. When I didn't see Scooter, either, the only thing left to do was find them and run them down.

I rolled my bicycle over the little ridge at the edge of the pond and plopped it on the ground. The thought of having to run after my pups . . . well . . . Finding a soft-looking spot with no weeds, I dropped beside my bike.

The breeze that came across the pond was cool and refreshing. After a couple of minutes, I felt a little better. Still on my back, I stuck the whistle in my mouth and blew three sharp blasts.

Scooter would show up first—he always did. So, I dug in my pocket, found one of his doggie treats, and put it on my stomach. It felt good to close my eyes and let the fresh breeze off the pond sweep over my sweaty face.

It wasn't long before little paws came rustling through the grass. I expected to see Scooter flying toward me, so it was a surprise to see Button. When he got to me, he didn't even stop to sniff the doggie treat on my stomach—he went straight for my face. Button was all over me. He leaped from one side to the other. He licked my face, and he almost knocked the air out of me when he bounced on my stomach.

Between his wet tongue sloshing me and pond water dropping off him, I felt like I was going to drown.

Hot and tired and sweaty and wet, I still couldn't help but laugh. He loved for me to lie on the ground with him. Licking me in the face was about the neatest thing in the whole world. His tail wagged so hard and fast, it felt like I'd been hit with a stick.

During all the laughing and playing and trying to protect myself, I realized Scooter hadn't shown up yet. Tucking Button under one arm, I whistled. When Scooter still didn't show up, I scrambled to my feet.

The coyote was no place in sight. I blew the whistle a few more times, then started around the pond to look for him. Button and I struggled to the crest of the dam and looked around.

We finally spotted Scooter out in the middle of the alfalfa field, running first one way and then the other. Watching the way he was acting, I could tell that he'd heard the whistle. It was like he was searching all over, trying to find me— only he couldn't.

I smiled and blew the whistle again.

The shrill sound cut through the morning air. But it was only half a whistle—it stopped short. My heart stopped.

Up the hill—beyond Scooter—was a soft cloud of dust. A blue pickup truck sat near our driveway. There was a metal box on the back. It was already open.

I saw the dogs. Sleek and streamlined, five of them shot under the fence. They streaked across the plowed wheat field like arrows pointed at a target. They were aimed right at Scooter.

Chapter 24

Scooter saw me.

The greyhounds saw Scooter.

Sucking in a huge gulp of air, I blew the whistle again. Ears flat against his head, Scooter sprinted toward me. He was a lot closer to the pond and me than the hounds were to him. Still, his short little puppy legs seemed no match for the greyhounds'.

"Come on, Scooter! Come on, boy!" I stuck a hand in my pocket, acting like I was going for one of his treats.

A glimmer of hope raced across my spine as I watched him run. He could make it! The way he was moving and as close as he was, he could get to me before the dogs got to him.

But what if that didn't stop the dogs? What if

they just kept coming? I couldn't fight them off. And what about Button? I reached down and swooped him up.

There had to be someplace safe. Someplace where the hounds couldn't get to Button or Scooter—or me.

Scooter was almost to us. The greyhounds were almost to the edge of the alfalfa. Once they hit the alfalfa field . . .

A tree!

My head whipped to the right. The closest trees were at the channel where the two creeks came together, clear down at the far end of the pond. The ones closest to us were cottonwoods. They were big and tall, but there were no low limbs—nothing I could reach. My heart pounded in my ears as I scanned the creek.

Scooter hit my leg. He jumped at my pocket and my hand, trying to get his treat. With only one free hand, there wasn't time to cradle him in my arm like I usually did. I grabbed him by the scruff of his neck. He let out a little yelp. Ignoring him, I took a trembling stride toward the trees. The greyhounds were already in the alfalfa.

147

The trees were too far. We'd never make it.

Something stirred in the back of my mind. Coyote . . . pond dam . . . The dam!

In the blink of an eye, I darted over the edge of the bank toward the water. Out of sight from the greyhounds, I raced around the water's edge, jumped the pile of driftwood at the corner, and shot straight to the center of the dam.

Still dangling by the scruff of his neck, Scooter wiggled and struggled. I held him out at arms length and squeezed Button tight against my chest. Then all three of us dived into the tin-horn. There was a musty smell—a mix of pond water and stale moss. Pulling myself along on one elbow, I worked us deeper into the long dark tube.

The pipe sloped downward from the pond toward the stream. Crawling downhill wasn't all that hard. So as quick as I could, I struggled until we were about in the middle of the long pipe. Once there, I froze. If we didn't move . . . if we didn't make a sound . . .

Scooter and Button couldn't understand. Scooter's little paws made scratching sounds as he tried to crawl away from me. Button started whining.

Somehow, in the tight space, I managed to get Button up beside my head. I held him down with my chin and got hold of Scooter with my left hand. Sure I had a good grip on him, I dug and pulled out a handful of doggie treats. Knowing the way he was when it came to food, I gripped his neck even tighter. If he latched onto my hand, I couldn't help but yell. I'd make more noise than the pups. Quick as I could, I laid them out.

Scooter quit trying to get away from me. Once he was busy eating, I pulled him back to the right side of my head.

I held each of them and made them lie down. Scooter gobbled his doggie treats, and Button entertained himself by licking my face.

All this happened in a matter of seconds. And when we were settled, the only thing I could do was hold my breath, hold my pups, and pray that the hounds didn't find us.

I could see light and a puddle of water at the far end of the tinhorn. Any second, I expected to see the sharp nose and long teeth of a grey-hound. How could I fight one off? How could I keep him away from my pups and my face?

I couldn't see behind me. In my mind's eye, I could picture a dog finding us from that direction. He'd clamber into the end of the pipe and come sliding down toward us. I wouldn't even see him coming. Maybe I could hear him. I knew I would be able to feel him as he bit and ripped at my feet and legs, trying to get past me and get at my coyote.

But there were no sounds. After a long time, I expected to hear the man's voice, yelling at his dogs, trying to get them to come back to him.

But that sound never came, either.

I couldn't tell how long we lay in the dark pipe. We waited an eternity. And when I thought we had surely waited long enough for the wolf hunter and his hounds to give up and go back to the truck—I waited longer.

Then, when I *knew* it had been long enough and we were finally safe—I waited even longer.

Chapter 25

The pups heard the sound first. On either side of me, their heads popped up and their ears perked. I held them tight. They wiggled and squirmed to get away from my hold. Still terrified that it was the greyhounds, I couldn't relax my grasp.

"Brad?"

The voice was faint—the sound of my name so far off and muffled that I wasn't sure I had really heard it.

The pups wanted free. I raised my head and squeezed them against each other and against my face.

"Brad? Brad? Where are you?"

It wasn't until Daddy's voice echoed through the pipe that I finally felt safe. He called my name over and over again. Each time the voice sounded closer. I tried to back out of the pipe but couldn't make it uphill crawling backward. Each time Button and Scooter heard him, their tails started wagging. On either side of my head, they whacked my ears and face until I almost felt dizzy. They were tired of being all cramped up in the dark pipe. They wanted out.

I held Button by his hind leg with one hand and Scooter's hind leg with the other. Shoving with my toes and using my elbows, we crawled down the long, dark tube until my head was in the sunlight.

"Brad? Brad?"

I stopped at the end of the pipe. There was no way to get out—to get past the puddle of water and still hold my pups at the same time.

"Dad. I'm down here. Are the dogs gone?"

"They're gone. It's safe. Where are you?"

I let go of Scooter and Button. They shot from the end of the pipe. Button landed smack in the water puddle and never broke stride. Scooter managed to miss it by pausing a second and jumping to the side. But before I could so much as blink, both were gone.

The puddle wasn't all that big. Still, hanging upside down from the end of the tinhorn, there was really no way for me to get around it. I ended up having to stick my left hand down to hold myself. It got wet clear up to the elbow and my left leg was soaked from my knee down to my tennis shoe. I was so wet, I sloshed when I walked.

"Dad. I'm down here. Where are you?"

Daddy appeared at the top of the dam. I rushed to him and hugged him as hard as I could. He hugged me back. Then he held me at arm's length. I could see the worry on his face.

"Are you all right, Brad? Are you hurt?"

"I'm fine. There was this pack of dogs and they were after Scooter and . . ."

The words stuck in my throat when I looked up and saw the blue truck still parked by our mailbox. A trembling finger pointed.

"Dad! It's . . . it's still there!"

"It's okay, Brad." Daddy wrapped an arm around me. "It's okay. The dogs are locked in the back. Mr. Bell has them closed up in the box. He's the one who told us about it. He's helping us try to find you, too."

"But . . . but, Daddy . . ."

"It's okay, son. You're safe. Your pups are safe. Everything's fine."

Daddy turned toward the trees where the two creeks joined to form the pond. He stretched his lips tight and stuck his little fingers at the corners of his mouth. The loud, shrill whistle cut through the air like a knife.

Scooter streaked toward us. He plowed into the side of my leg so hard, he almost knocked me down. There was one doggie treat left in my pocket. Scooter caught it in midair, swallowed it in one gulp, then took off to explore some more.

Daddy whistled again. A man, dressed in a blue work shirt and jeans, appeared at the head of the right channel. When he saw Daddy and me, he waved. Then he cupped a hand beside his mouth and turned toward the other creek.

"Mrs. McBride," he called. "Mrs. McBride, Darrel found him. The boy's all right. They're at the pond."

The man started jogging around the bank toward us. On the opposite side, Adelee appeared at the edge of the other creek. She had on her soccer uniform and shoes. When she saw us, she started running.

Adelee got to us first. Just about the time she leaped over the pile of driftwood at the corner of the pond, I saw Mama and Mr. Bigbee. Mama was carrying Casey.

I'd seen Adelee look worried before—once, when she wasn't sure if she was going to make the soccer team and again the morning she had to take her driving test. But in my whole life, I'd never seen her worried about me. She sprinted up beside Daddy and hugged me.

"He's fine," Daddy said.

For an instant Adelee almost smiled. Then she let me go, jabbed both fists against her hips, and glared at me.

"Where have you been?" she demanded.

Before I could say anything, she slugged me on the arm.

"You scared us half to death," she sniffed. "I can't believe you'd scare us like that. We thought you fell in the pond . . . we thought you—"

She broke off, sniffling.

Mr. Bell got there before Mama and Mr. Big-bee. I guess I expected—no, *wanted*—him to be the villain. Before he came up, I had a clear picture in my mind's eye.

He would be young. Not as young as me, but young. He would have long hair, a scraggly beard and mustache, and shifty eyes that made him look sneaky.

But Mr. Bell was older than Daddy, although not as old as Mr. Holdbrook. His eyes were gentle. He looked like he was holding back tears.

"I'm sorry, boy." His voice quivered when he spoke. "You must have been lying down or over the edge of the bank. I didn't see you—I swear. I didn't see you until I'd already let the dogs out of the back. I didn't even know you were around or the coyote was yours or . . . or—"

He made a loud gulping sound. "When I couldn't find you, well I was scared that you'd fallen in the pond and . . . and—Lord, boy, I'm so sorry."

He turned his face away and used a sleeve to wipe his eyes. Mama and the others got to us. Once sure I was all right, Mr. Bigbee reached out and ruffled my hair. When the rest of us started for home, he went back to his tractor.

Daddy carried my bicycle for me. Button and Scooter scampered all around us as we marched up the hill and across the plowed field. Mama didn't say much. Adelee just glared at me.

Mr. Bell was kind of a disappointment. I wanted him to be mean and rough and uncaring. It would have been a lot easier to hate him—him and all the other coyote hunters.

Trouble was, he was one of the nicest men I ever met. He must have told me how sorry he was a dozen times as we walked up the hill. "I wasn't even hunting today," he said. "Dogs have been cramped-up in the pen for a long while. I was taking them over to Harry Jantz's farm so they could run and get some exercise. We only hunt in the winter. But I saw that coyote . . . and . . . and . . ."

Remembering the day I found Scooter, I glanced toward the hill above Tony Hollow Creek. "You hunt in the winter so the dogs won't hurt the pups, right?"

Mr. Bell stopped. "Wish I could say that was the reason." He cleared his throat. "Nobody wants to hurt a baby. Not even a baby coyote.

Truth is, we hunt in the winter 'cause the grass is flattened down, the wheat is still short, and it's easier for the hounds to see what they're chasing. Roger Hick's dogs were the ones who ran across the babies. He wasn't too happy about it, but dogs are dogs and—" Mr. Bell broke off and started walking again.

When we got to his truck, he gave me a big hug and told me again how scared he'd been.

"By the way," he said, frowning. "Where *were* you hiding?"

I started to answer, then stopped. I didn't want him to know about the hiding place. "Thanks for getting my mom and dad," I smiled, changing the subject. "I was tired from pushing my bicycle across the plowed ground. That's why you didn't see me. I guess it was partly my fault."

Mr. Bell patted my shoulder. "No, son. I should have been more careful. 'Course, I never heard of anyone having a coyote as a pet. The other guys might think I'm crazy, but I'll tell them about it. I promise nothing like that will happen again." With that, he hopped in his truck and left.

Back home, Daddy drove Adelee to soccer

practice. She was already forty-five minutes late. I put my pups in the backyard and locked the gate. Mama plopped Casey in his high chair and fed him some cornflakes.

Alone in my room, I remembered the male coyote, and that tinhorn. How he tried to hide but found it full of water. How the dogs chased him. How horribly he died.

I started trembling all over. I didn't cry, but no matter how hard I tried, I just couldn't stop shaking.

Chapter 26

🐾

The first Saturday in July, Nolan and I finally got to go fishing. We met at the pond, just about the time the sun was coming up.

We spent the whole day there, fishing and talking. Mama had sent a couple of sandwiches and some chips for lunch. We ended up with twelve perch, seven largemouth bass, and a catfish. A little before dark, we headed to Nolan's. After we cleaned them, his mother fried them up for supper. They were delicious!

When we finished eating, my parents came over to drive me home. Only they got to visiting with the Bigbees, then ended up playing cards for a while. It was really late by the time we got to the house.

I was totally pooped. A whole day fishing and staying up late . . . I slept like a log.

The next morning I was still half asleep when I staggered in and plopped down in the kitchen chair. As usual, Adelee was the last one to come for breakfast. She slid into her chair, but instead of eating she just glared at me.

I tried to ignore her. That usually worked. She just kept staring.

"What?" I asked, finally.

Adelee just glared.

I took another bite of bacon.

Adelee didn't say anything.

"What?" I repeated.

"You didn't hear it?"

"Hear what?"

"Last night."

"I was asleep. I was so tired, I didn't hear a thing."

"The coyotes. Scooter." She rolled her eyes. "All night long, they kept howling and your coyote howled back."

I glanced at Mama, who was feeding Casey his cereal. She nodded.

I remembered Button lying down next to me but couldn't recall if I'd brought Scooter in or not. Guess I hadn't.

"You're going to have to do something with that stupid thing." Adelee squeezed a piece of bacon so hard, it shattered before she got it to her plate. "I can't get a bit of rest with him howling all night. You're going to have to keep him quiet."

I nodded.

"I'll take care of it. No worries."

I wasn't worried, either. All I needed to do was remember to bring Scooter inside. The only reason I forgot last night was because I was so tired.

Maybe I should have worried.

For the rest of the summer, it was an on-and-off battle with Scooter to get him to bed.

Lots of nights, the coyotes didn't howl. Scooter and Button would romp and play in the yard, running and chasing and wearing themselves out. As soon as I opened my bedroom window, they'd race over so I could pull them inside. The battle was off. There was no problem at all.

But if the coyotes howled or if Scooter so much as smelled something in the air, the battle was on.

Most times, the coyotes' howls sounded more like yapping. Sometimes a whole bunch would get started and Scooter would race to the back fence and add his voice to the chorus. Button would even join them at times. He didn't yap like a coyote. He stood really stiff with his tail sticking straight up behind him. Then he lifted his head high.

When Button howled, it was a howl, starting deep in his throat and growing louder and louder. Instead of little yips, his howl would go as much as twenty to thirty seconds. Once he'd told the coyotes they better not bother him, he scampered to the window and wanted in. He sounded brave, but acted like such a sissy.

Scooter was totally different. He yapped and called when the coyotes howled. When they quit, he kept it up, trying to get them to answer. Sometimes he sounded like four or five coyotes. He managed to change his voice and the pitch or the way he howled or yapped. All by himself, he could make enough noise for a whole pack.

When he wasn't howling, he tried to dig under the fence. Every morning I would go out and fill in his holes with rocks or wire and dirt. At first, I tried to go out and get him. I'd call his name and dig into my pocket, like I had a treat. He'd just ignore me.

When the coyotes were around, Scooter didn't like being dragged to the house. A couple of times, he even snapped and tried to bite my hand. That wasn't like Scooter at all. Usually I didn't have to worry about getting bitten. Unless I got him cornered just right, Scooter had no problem outrunning or out-dodging me. We scampered around the yard until I was so tired I didn't care. And as soon as I quit chasing him, he went back to his yapping and howling, trying to get the other coyotes to answer him.

One morning at breakfast, Daddy mentioned how Scooter wanted to be with the other coyotes—how he missed being with his own kind.

I listened to him, but I tried *not* to hear. I didn't want to hear.

Despite the howling, Scooter was more dog than coyote. That's how I had it figured. I mean, after all, he'd been raised with Button. He even

164

slept in a bed. What coyote would do something like that?

But by the middle of September, I finally gave up.

We moved Scooter to the pen out behind the barn. It was only at night, though. The pen was far enough from the house that his yapping didn't keep us awake at nights. First thing in the morning, I let him come into the backyard with Button. That way, while we were at school, they could play and keep each other company.

In the afternoons I would get a pocketful of doggie treats, the playground whistle, and my bicycle. After the scare I got from the grey-hounds, we didn't venture off our own place.

I was amazed at how Scooter had grown. For a long time, both pups were about the same size. But lately Scooter had gotten a whole bunch bigger than Button. Button was still small and clumsy. Scooter was big and sleek.

One Friday, in the middle of October, Scooter didn't come when I whistled. I rode my bike to the last place I saw him, but he wasn't there. So I spent the next thirty minutes riding all over the pasture, blowing the whistle and calling his name.

The longer I called and hunted, the more scared I got. Finally I decided that he had gone home, so I rode back to the house to see. Scooter wasn't in the backyard. I looked in his pen. He wasn't there, either. Terror raced across my spine when I looked down toward the wheat field. I closed my eyes.

In that instant, I could see the two coyotes. The truck. The greyhounds. The chase. Then the fight as the dogs snarled and bit and ripped and . . . I could see the babies, and I could hear the little coyote's mournful cry when the one he nudged with his nose wouldn't wake up.

Shaking, I forced my eyes open. Scooter wasn't there.

I looked one way, then the other. There were no pickup trucks. No hounds.

Still shaking, I ran for help.

Daddy and I got in his car and drove back behind the house. Mama and the others got in her car and started around the section.

I can't ever remember being so scared. What if we couldn't find him? What if the coyote hunters were around? Tomorrow was Saturday. What if Scooter was still lost—alone?

Daddy and I searched every inch of our eighty acres. Scooter wasn't there.

"We may not find him, Brad," Daddy said as we started back to the house. "He's a coyote. A wild animal. You know how he's been yapping and howling at the other coyotes. He's almost grown. Maybe he left to be with his own."

I swallowed the lump in my throat.

"Scooter wouldn't do that, Daddy. He's my pup. He loves Button. He just wouldn't up and leave us."

"I know he loves you, Brad. You've been good to him and fed him and played with him. You even let him sleep with you. Still, Brad, he's a coyote. He's not a puppy anymore. All animals—dogs, cats, coyotes, even people—all animals need their own kind. I mean, you enjoy school. You enjoy your friends. Would you be happy if you had to spend your whole life with just your dog and Scooter?"

I started to answer, but Daddy didn't give me the chance.

"No, you wouldn't. It's the same with Scooter.

167

You've got to face the fact that you may never see him again. And it's not because he doesn't love you."

Suddenly, I saw Adelee walking up the hill toward us, waving her arms. I rolled my window down. Adelee smiled.

"We got the little stinker," she called.

"Where?"

She pointed toward the highway. "He was by the road. It's a wonder he didn't get run over. He was just standing in the bar-ditch sniffing and looking around. If he'd tried to cross the road . . ." She stopped what she was saying and shook her head.

Daddy parked his car. The instant Daddy turned the motor off, I jumped out to check on my coyote.

Suddenly, a hand grabbed my arm. Daddy smiled at me. "Brad." His voice was as soft and gentle as his smile. "I know it's something you don't want to hear—something you don't want to think about. But you might have to let Scooter go."

We sat there for only a second or two. It seemed like a lifetime.

Chapter 27

I didn't sleep at all that night. My coyote was back home and safe. Button was snuggled up in the crook of my leg. Despite the scare, everything was all right. I couldn't get to sleep, though. I kept tossing and turning. My stomach hurt. My back and legs ached. I guess all the worrying I had done got me more upset than I thought.

Maybe if we can keep Scooter through the winter . . . maybe he'll forget about the other coyotes. Maybe he'll be a people coyote like Mr. Holdbrook's Scooter. If we can just make it a little while longer.

I kicked the covers back and ran to the bathroom.

* * *

"Flu."

That's what the doctor in the emergency room told my parents early Saturday morning.

"Good thing you brought him in," the doctor went on. "He's got 103.8 temperature. You say he threw up a lot last night?"

Daddy nodded. "A whole lot."

"Probably close to being dehydrated, too. We can take care of that."

I ended up getting a shot and a bunch of pills I had to take. By the time I got home, I was already feeling a little better, but not much.

Mama brought me fruit juice. Daddy drove to town and came back with a chocolate milk shake for me. Even Adelee was nice—she brought her little TV into my room and hooked it up.

"You'll probably give me your flu," she said, talking real snottylike. "If I get sick, I want my TV back." I opened one eye and peeked up at her. Instead of that smart-aleck look, she was smiling. She really felt sorry for me. Adelee was hardly ever nice to me, or at least it seemed that way. It was good to know that she actually cared.

Mama kept bringing me juice and water. I'd drink them fast so I could go back to sleep. Only as soon as I drank one glass, she'd bring me a glass of something else. I drank enough to float a battleship.

When I got out of bed and moved around a little, I felt a whole lot better than I had all day. I waddled off toward the kitchen. About halfway there, I noticed how dark it seemed outside. It was almost night—time to feed the pups and get Scooter out to his pen. So I doubled back to my room, slipped on a pair of sweatpants and my moccasins.

I had the dry food in Button's and Scooter's bowls and was just mixing in the canned meat, when Mama spotted me at the kitchen sink.

"What do you think you're doing out of bed, young man?"

"Got to feed the pups. Put Scooter out in his pen."

Mama came over and nudged me away from the bowls. "No way you're going outside as sick as you are. Go back to bed. I'll feed them."

"Rhonda," Daddy called from the playroom. "It's the phone. The Motts."

Adelee came over, balancing Casey on her hip. Adelee picked up Button's bowl and motioned to

171

the door. "I'll feed them. Open the door. I'll come back for the other one."

"Do you want me to take Casey?" I asked.

"No, you'll probably give him the flu."

"Wait. You have to take Scooter's bowl first. If you put Button's down, Scooter grabs it and you can't get him out of the yard."

She put Button's bowl back on the cabinet and picked up the other one. "Can you get the gate for me?" She didn't even wait for an answer. "No, you can't go outside. I'll bring Scooter through the house."

Adelee leaned through the back door and showed Scooter his bowl. He shot to her like a bullet and started bouncing against her leg. She kept his bowl up and out of his reach, then headed for the front door. While she went on the right side of the couch, I moved around on the left. That way I could have the door opened for her before she and Casey got there.

"He's real *grabby* about his food," I reminded her. "When you get him in the pen and set the bowl down, don't stand there and hold on to it. Get your hand out of the way."

Adelee didn't answer, but she nodded her head. Adelee had never helped feed the pups before. As I watched her, I couldn't help but smile. Maybe she wasn't so bad, after all. I mean . . . for a big sister.

I went back to the kitchen and got Button's bowl. Mama was talking on one phone and Daddy on the other. I got Button's food and motioned toward the back door. Mama nodded, then slapped her hand over the mouthpiece on the phone. "Don't go outside, though."

"I'll just set it on the back porch." I nodded. "Okay?"

"Okay." Mama started talking once more.

I slid Button's bowl out on the concrete and waited just long enough to give him a quick scratch behind his ears. Once back inside, I stood in the doorway between the playroom and the kitchen.

The Motts had been Mama and Daddy's best friends back in Chicago. I liked them, too. Their daughter, Kerry, was a year younger than me. We used to fight a lot when we were little. But right before we moved down here, I couldn't help but notice that she was getting kind of cute.

Standing between Mama and Daddy at the doorway, I could pick up most of the conversation. The Motts were planning to drive down to Oklahoma during fall break. I smiled to myself, wondering if Kerry was even cuter than the last time I saw her. I bet she'll love Scooter and Button. I bet . . .

The blood-chilling scream that came when our front door burst open sent a chill racing up my spine.

It was Casey. He was screaming and bawling, and I couldn't tell if he was hurt or scared or . . .

As sick and weak as I was, it only took two strides for me to reach the living room. Adelee stood in the doorway. Casey had both arms around her neck, squeezing so tight, her eyes almost seemed to bug out. Casey screamed louder when he saw me. Adelee seemed a little pale, but she was calm as could be.

"Brad, do me a favor and bring a couple of old towels from the kitchen." Her voice was surprisingly relaxed. "I need to get to the sink, but I'm afraid I'll drip on the carpet."

Adelee turned a little bit and opened the door wider.

There was blood everywhere!

There was blood on her pants and shirt. There was blood on Casey's clothes and on his little arm. There was blood dripping on the porch.

A knot drew up in my stomach at the sight. When I realized what had happened, the knot tightened.

"Scooter."

Chapter 28

It wasn't long after Adelee and Daddy got back from the emergency room that she came and sat on my bed.

I never felt so miserable in my life. It was all my fault. In a way, I hoped she would be mean to me—even hit me or something. Maybe that would take some of the guilt away about my coyote tearing her up.

"Knock it off!" she snapped.

I pulled the pillow off my head and rolled over to look at her.

"I'm sorry," I sniffed. "It's all my fault."

"Oh, shut up!"

Adelee sounded mean, but she smiled at me. "It was my fault. I've heard you and Daddy talk about how Scooter is with his food. You even reminded me when I walked out the door with him. I knew better."

"I was so scared." I wiped my nose with the sleeve of my pajamas. "There was so much blood I . . . I thought it was Casey . . . or both of you . . . and . . . and . . . I'm so sorry, Adelee."

"I'm fine, Brad. Really. When I set the food bowl down, Scooter jumped in the middle of it, with his front paws, and growled at me. I should have remembered. But he sounded like he was just playing, instead of really growling. He looked so cute, I just reached down to pet him and . . .

"It was my own stupid fault. Now would you shut up and stop that bawling?"

I sat up in bed. Adelee moved beside me and hugged me. I hugged her back.

"Stitches?"

Adelee showed me her hand. "Nine. But you can't see them because they wrapped everything." There was white gauze around her hand and up her arm a little ways. "It only took three for my hand, but he had to put six on my wrist and arm."

"Was it bad? Did the stitches really hurt?"

Adelee looked around, as if making sure no one was watching or listening.

"I was scared to death about the stitches," she whispered. "I'd never had stitches before. Where Scooter bit me, well, it really didn't hurt all that much at first. After we sat around in the emergency waiting room for about forty-five minutes, it got to throbbing pretty good. Then this nurse came in, took us to a little room and cleaned where he bit me with this iodine stuff. That was pretty rough. But the stitches"—she let out a little laugh—"after all the worrying I did about them, shoot, the stitches were nothing. The doctor went around the edge of each bite with this little needle and deadened it. Other than feeling him push and a little jar when the needle popped through the skin—I didn't feel a thing."

"Honest?"

Adelee nodded. "I swear. It didn't hurt at all." She gave me one more hug. "Come on. Let's go see what Mama's got for supper."

"I'm not hungry."

Adelee glared down her nose at me. "Come on, *Brat,* before I slap snot out of you."

It really wasn't a very nice thing to say. But the way Adelee said it—the way she smiled at me—well, it was the sweetest thing ever.

I didn't eat much. Mostly, I played with my plate and scooted stuff from one side to the other. My stomach felt awful, and just the smell of the food was enough to make me want to throw up. That—along with all the thoughts and feelings that raced through my head—well, I just wasn't hungry. Mama reached over and felt my forehead. She smiled. "I believe your temperature has broken." But about five minutes later, she felt me and frowned. "Think you better go back to your room?" I nodded, and while they finished supper, I curled up in my bed with a pillow on my stomach.

I didn't sleep, though. I couldn't. Even as sick as I was and as tired—the thoughts of what I had to do kept coming. I clutched the pillow tighter against my stomach.

Daddy came and sat down so gently on my bed that I hardly felt him.

"Brad," he whispered. "You awake?"

"I'm awake."

179

He cleared his throat, and scooted closer. "I think there's something we need to talk about. Something we need to discuss."

I sat up.

"We don't need to talk about it, Daddy." When the words came out, I fought hard to keep tears from following them. "I know what has to be done."

Daddy and I sat on the bed for a long, long time.

"It scared me so bad," I said finally. "When I heard Casey screaming and saw all the blood . . . Casey's just a little kid. He can't protect himself. And if we left Scooter in the pen all the time, well, he loves to play with Button. He wouldn't be happy. And . . . and . . ."

I broke off, staring down at the pillow clutched over my tummy.

After another long stretch of quiet, Daddy cleared his throat. "I've noticed how, the last three weeks or so, Scooter's been howling at the other coyotes. Remember when Mr. Holdbrook said how one of the coyotes he had just didn't adapt to living with people? How—"

"But he used to sleep with me and Button," I broke in. "He loved sleeping in the house or playing in my bedroom, and soccer. Adelee and I had so much fun playing soccer with him and . . ."

The tears started leaking out.

Daddy patted my leg. But he didn't say anything.

"I thought about just letting him out. He could run with the other coyotes on our place or on the Bigbees' farm. Sometimes he might drop by the house for food or just to say hi, and I could see him or play with him or . . ."

I started bawling. Daddy wrapped his arms around me.

After a while, I took a deep breath.

"But we can't do that, Daddy. We can't let him loose around here. Every time I think about it, I remember the coyote and the pond. When I close my eyes, I can see those hounds chasing him and catching him and how he fought . . ."

The words kept tumbling out. Rambling, scrambling over one another in a steady stream that just kept going and going. When I finished jabbering and crying and jabbering some more, Daddy squeezed me tight and sniffed.

"We'll figure out something, son. Something."

"I know, Daddy. I love him and I don't want to lose him, but I know Scooter can't stay."

Chapter 29

Mama caught the flu about two days after I did. Both of us stayed home for the rest of that week.

On Friday, ten days after Scooter bit Adelee, she got her stitches taken out. The wounds were red and puffy, but the doctor told us that it looked good. He promised that, after a while, she wouldn't be able to see the scars.

That Saturday I got up real early, brought Scooter into the backyard, and let him and Button play. I did fine until he crawled up in my lap and nuzzled my cheek. Then I had to fight to keep the tears back. Scooter felt it. He kissed my ear and the side of my face with his long, sloppy tongue.

About nine, Daddy loaded us all in the car, and we drove to the Wichita Mountain Wildlife

Refuge. Adelee, Mama, and Casey rode in the backseat. Daddy, Scooter, and I rode in the front. Scooter spent part of the time on my lap, looking out the window. After a while, he settled down and lay between us on the front seat.

The refuge was about fifty miles from our house. Daddy had heard about it from another teacher at school who always took her third graders there for a field trip.

Even before we got to the green sign that said MEDICINE PARK EXIT, we saw the mountains. I guess they weren't really big enough to be called mountains. But the way they just sort of popped up, out of the rolling plains and flat Oklahoma prairie . . . well, they sure looked like mountains.

We stopped at a store, just off the exit ramp, and everybody went to the rest room and got something to drink. I got a package of beef jerky for Scooter. He loved it.

The mountains were really neat, with enormous boulders and oak trees and cedars. In our yard, we had mostly Chinese elm. In the autumn, the leaves turned yellow or brown and fell off. But here, it was beautiful. The oak leaves were bright red and orange. The cedars threw in a splash of green. We went by two big lakes. Their water was blue and clear, instead of the dingy-brown of the farm ponds near us. A big mountain rose on our right. After we passed the lakes, the road forked and one went up the side of the mountain. Adelee wanted to drive up and see if it went clear to the top. Daddy promised that if there was time on the way home, we would.

We drove for quite a ways before we stopped at an enormous building. Even though it was kind of modern, it blended in with the rustic setting.

Daddy went inside. We didn't wait long. He came back and hopped in the car.

"Wrong place. This is the Visitors' Center. Ranger Headquarters is a ways farther. That's where we're supposed to meet Mr. Gardner."

There were a million things to see as we drove. A herd of bison crossed the road in front of us—one of them so close that I could have rolled the window down and patted his rump. Scooter kept hopping up and down on my lap and pushing on the glass with his paws.

About a mile from where we stopped, the road forked again. There were more lakes and thick stands of oaks with their bright fall colors glistening in the sun. After another six or seven miles, we came to a sign that said RANGER HEADQUARTERS.

Mr. Gardner met us in front of a big, redbrick building. A little shorter than Dad, he was stout and had a mustache.

I put Scooter down. He raced off and found a place to go to the bathroom. When I blew Mama's playground whistle and reached in my pocket, he shot right back to us.

We followed Mr. Gardner down the hill. Mama, Adelee, and Casey stopped at this little pen. There was a baby buffalo in it. Daddy, Mr. Gardner, and I went on to another pen. This one had chain-link wire and went back into the trees and rocks so far that I couldn't tell how big it was.

"Our holding pen," Mr. Gardner said, opening the gate. Scooter must have thought it was like the gate to our backyard. He trotted in to explore. "With animals that are being returned to the wild," Mr. Gardner went on, "we usually keep them here a couple of weeks. That way we can tell if they've got a chance or not."

"A chance?" I frowned.

Mr. Gardner nodded, but he didn't look at me. "Some animals can't survive in the wild. Lots of people want a bobcat or a mountain lion. Cats are cute when they're little, but like all animals, they mature and change. They'll have them de-clawed. We can't even *think* about taking a cat like that. No way they can hunt for themselves. Can't believe people are so thoughtless and stupid."

I ducked my head and he noticed the movement. Mr. Gardner gave out a little laugh.

"Not talking about you, boy. When your dad called on the phone, he told me about the coyote hunters. That pup wouldn't have lived without your help. Mostly, we get animals who have been hit by cars. Rescue agencies or licensed volunteers care for them until they recover. Get raccoons and squirrels, coyotes and badgers, even wounded deer that somebody found after a hunter left them for dead. Most of them do just fine."

Scooter was roaming and exploring way off in the trees. He was easy to see amid the bright colors. I thought I'd better whistle him back in.

A big, callused hand reached out and caught my arm.

I looked up. Mr. Gardner shook his head.

"Hang on, Brad. I think he's found her."

"Her?"

"Nakita." Mr. Gardner motioned with a nod of his head. I couldn't see what he was looking at. He pointed.

"There. About halfway into the trees and a little to the right. She's by that pile of rocks. Lady from Burkburnett brought her in day before yesterday. Found her about a month ago, alongside the turnpike. Vet in Wichita Falls set the leg without charge. She's healed up so well, you can't even tell it was broken."

"Excuse me, Mr. Gardner." Daddy said. "I can't see it, either. What are we talking about?"

"Nakita. Female coyote." Smiling, he pointed again. "She's older than your pup, Brad. Wait. I think he's got her spotted."

I saw Scooter disappear behind a rock but never saw another animal. All of a sudden, there was a whole bunch of squealing and snarling and yapping. Tail tucked, Scooter came flying through the trees toward us. When he reached me, he started jumping against my leg. I tried to pick him up, but every time I did, he hopped back out of my reach. Finally, I dug in my pocket and handed him a doggie treat. He swallowed it in one gulp, and tail wagging like a flag flopping in the breeze, he took off toward the trees again.

This time, he didn't come back.

We went outside the pen. Mr. Gardner latched the gate behind us. We stood and watched for a while. Once I saw Scooter come flying out from behind the rocks. The female coyote was hot on his heels. Then he spun and chased her. It kind of reminded me of the coyotes I had watched a long, long time ago. Then she chased him again, only she spotted us and hid behind the rocks. This time she didn't come out. Scooter stood beneath an enormous oak, watching her.

Daddy and Mr. Gardner started back up the hill. I stayed. When I leaned against the gate, it rattled a bit. Scooter looked at me. His ears flattened against his head and he wagged his tail.

I wanted him to come racing to me. I wanted him to jump against the fence until I opened it and then bounce against my leg, asking for a treat. One last time, I wanted to pet him and hug him and feel him wiggle in my arms as his tongue lapped my cheek. He stood, watching, for a long time. His eyes never left me.

A gust of wind rustled the tree limbs. A single, bright, orange leaf drifted down and brushed his ear as it fluttered to the ground. He sniffed it, took one look at me—hesitated for only an instant—then turned back to the female coyote. My heart sank as she bolted from the rocks and they both disappeared toward the far side of the pen.

Head low and feet dragging the ground, I followed Daddy and Mr. Gardner up the hill.

"I'll be honest with you," Mr. Gardner said at our car. "I really think he's going to be all right. In about two weeks, I'll give you a call. I still have your number on my desk. You can come down and watch us release them. We'll let them go in the North Pasture."

"What's that?" I asked.

"It's a special place in the refuge. It's away from cars and people. Don't need to worry about coyote hunters, either. There are more than 59,000 acres in the refuge. In the North Pasture alone, there are 33,400 acres. There's more than enough room for him to roam and plenty of rabbits and rats for him to eat."

I leaned across Daddy. "What if he can't hunt or survive in the wild?"

"Not much chance of a zoo taking him, Brad. Coyotes are plentiful and not that popular in zoos. As far as some animal shelter . . . well, the ones I know about are pretty full. They don't have enough people or enough money. Might be kinder if you had him put to sleep." He winked at me. "But I don't think you need to worry. I think he'll be just fine."

Mama leaned forward and peeked over Daddy's shoulder.

"Will you call us, Mr. Gardner? One way or the other, will you call so Brad can decide?"

With a finger, Mr. Gardner traced an *X* over his chest.

"Promise. You got my word on it."

Chapter 30

We stopped at the prairie-dog town on the way back home. Casey wanted to go chase them, and Mama, Daddy, and Adelee had to keep dragging him back under the wooden pole fence.

I didn't get out.

We drove up Mount Scott. Sure enough, the road went clear to the top. Mama, Daddy, Adelee, and Casey got out to go look and climb on the rocks.

I stayed in the car.

Mama came back and said how pretty all the different colors were and that you could see a long ways.

I stayed in the car.

Daddy came back and told me to quit sitting

on my butt and that I'd have fun and feel better if I played on the rocks for a while.

I stayed in the car.

Adelee came back and threatened to slap snot out of me. Then she yanked the car door open and dragged me out by one arm.

I stayed *out of* the car.

Mama and Daddy were right. The view from the top of Mount Scott was really neat. There were more mountains to our west. Autumn orange, red, yellow, and green splashed together in a whirlwind of color. There were towns, and even with a haze in the distance, I could see forever. Climbing on the rocks took some concentration. And for a while—just a little while— following Adelee and Daddy over the enormous boulders kept my mind off my coyote.

Mama and Daddy found a place at the very top, where the road circled around, that had lots of big rocks but no cliffs to fall off. Adelee went with them and they let Casey climb and play. They stayed really close to him, because he was still little and clumsy as could be.

I went to the other side of the mountain and

found a big rock. Even far away and with the wind sweeping over the top of the mountain, I could hear Casey. His giggles and happy squeals cut through the air as crisp and clear as a bell. For a second it almost made me smile.

Below, I spotted the road that went to the ranger headquarters. Following it as it wound through the mountains and bright fall trees like a silvery stream, I still couldn't see the buildings. It was just too far away. I kept looking, though. Kept staring off in the distance, as if I might catch a glimpse of . . . of something.

A dull pain kept gnawing at my insides. A hurt that sort of bent me over and made my shoulders slump. An emptiness that just wouldn't go away.

I told Mama about it after she put Casey to bed that night. She smiled and brushed my hair from my forehead. Her hands were always so soft and gentle.

She told me it was natural to feel that way. She said as how I loved Scooter and he was the first pet I ever had, and any time you lose someone or something you love, that empty feeling comes. She told me that after a while, the hurt wouldn't be so bad.

A couple of days later, Daddy noticed me moping around. He told me pretty much the same thing.

Adelee dragged me out in the yard to play soccer. It just wasn't the same without Scooter.

One day, when no one was watching, I noticed Button standing out by the back fence. He put his paws on the chain link and stood there for a long time, watching Scooter's pen. He missed Scooter, too. Watching him made me cry. I wiped the tears off before I went back inside.

Button snuggled at night. He could tell how sad I was and how much I missed my other pup. Each night, when I lifted him through my bedroom window, he tried to cheer me up by wiggling all over the place and licking me in the face.

It made me laugh. Only, as soon as I shoved him down and made him be still so we could get some sleep, that gnawing hurt came back again.

Mr. Gardner kept his promise. Two weeks to the day after we left Scooter, he called. He talked to Daddy first, then Daddy gave the phone to me. Scooter was doing great. He and the female coyote got along fantastically. He told me there was no need to worry about him surviving, either. Scooter was "a real champ" when it came to catching mice and rats and rabbits. He could make it in the wild—"hang right in there with the best of them."

Tomorrow morning—Sunday—they were going to release them into the North Pasture. He told me it would make me feel better to see it.

I wanted to go. I wanted to see, for myself, that Scooter was all right and happy. But there was a part of me that tightened up like a hard knot in a shoestring. What if Scooter came racing to me? What if he wagged his tail and bounced against my leg for a treat from my pocket or if he wanted me to hold him so he could kiss me with that wet tongue?

With all my heart, I wanted to go. I just couldn't.

Daddy was back on the couch. He had a pillow clutched to his stomach. Adelee's door squeaked when it flew open. Guess she was running to the bathroom to throw up again.

Telling Mr. Gardner that the family had the flu and no one felt like driving down there . . . well, it made a good excuse. Even if it wasn't really the truth. I thanked him for calling and told him that I wanted to remember Scooter just like he was when we let him go in the pen.

In February I got mad at Adelee for trying to pet Scooter when he was eating. And I got mad at Casey for always walking around with food in his grubby, little hands. I even got a little mad at God for giving Scooter to me, only to take him away. Mostly, I was mad at me. He was just a coyote. Why couldn't I forget about him?

I confronted Mama. Told her that she was wrong and I couldn't forget Scooter.

"I never in my life told you that you'd forget Scooter!"

Mama was always soft and gentle. It startled me when she snapped at me.

"You never should forget him. You loved him. He was the first pet you ever had. There's no way you could ever forget!" Her look softened. She took my face and held it between her hands. "What I said was that, in time, it wouldn't hurt so much. I didn't tell you, you would forget."

In April, Mr. Gardner called again. He told us that one of the rangers had spotted Scooter and Nakita in the valley where they released them. They had their first litter of pups. He said they were the healthiest litter the ranger had seen in a long time.

In June, Daddy got a call. Nathan Holdbrook wanted to tell us that his father had passed away. He said the funeral was already over and that he called to tell us how much his father had enjoyed the visit to his old place. He said that his father knew we would take care of it and love living there as much as he had.

For some reason—I don't know why—I went out on the front porch. I sat down in the old rocker. It was dark, but I could still see the glow from the sun. It turned the clouds in the western sky all pink and red and purple. I remembered Mr. Holdbrook sitting in this same old chair, saying as how his coyotes were the best and worst pets he ever had. I remember wondering, not understanding, what he meant.

But now I knew.

I did pretty well until autumn. Working hard in school and trying to make good grades kept me busy. Nolan and I went fishing a few times. Dad and Mr. Bigbee even drove us down to Lake Texhoma to go Striper fishing. We caught a bunch of Striper bass, and all four of us had fun talking and just being together. Staying busy helped keep me from thinking about Scooter.

Then, one afternoon in late October, Dad and I went out to rake leaves. When we finished, he went inside to wash up for supper. I sat down in the old rocker to rest a minute, while waiting for him to get out of the bathroom. Adelee let Button out. He ran to sniff at the holly bushes, like maybe there was a bird hiding there.

Something brushed my cheek. I leaned away from it, figuring it was a bug or wasp. A leaf rested on my shirt. I reached down, held it between my thumb and forefinger to look at it.

It was an oak leaf. It was bright orange.

For a second, I wondered about it. Most of the leaves around here were yellow or brown. The only place I'd seen bright orange and red leaves was . . .

In the distance, the train whistle sounded at the road crossing near Pioneer School. A pack of coyotes answered. It was a mournful sound—but at the same time, free and wild.

Button raced back to the edge of the porch. His tail went straight up on one end. His head and neck stretched straight up on the other. He howled—long and loud. When he stopped, the coyotes answered back.

Tail tucked, Button raced to me and climbed up in my lap. I couldn't help but laugh.

I looked down across the valley. There wasn't enough light in the evening sky to see any coyotes. When the pack called, their voices came from the other direction. But in the shadows—there by Tony Hollow Creek—I could see the two coyotes I'd watched so long ago. I could see them romping and playing chase. I could see them—the big strong one and the little pudgy one—as they snuggled together.

I knew Scooter was safe. I could almost see him, the female coyote, and their new babies romping and playing among the rocks and autumn leaves.

Twirling the bright orange leaf by the stem, I smiled, then let it go.

Scooter was okay. So was I.

But even to this day, in autumn, when the leaves turn, I remember.